Sheep, Goats and Soap

Tim Simpson, head of the Art Investment Fund at White's Bank, is back in hot water as he and his wife Sue pursue a trail of murder, deception, and violent greed against a brooding background of Pre-Raphaelite artistic inheritance and illusion spun between London, Japan and a Hastings clifftop. Sheep, goats and soap are the last things Tim believes he is seeking, yet the enduring symbolism of the Pre-Raphaelites dogs his every step.

Sheep are innocent creatures needing an attentive shepherd. Holman Hunt painted them in canvases intended as a stern warning to us all.

Goats are credited with venal, cunning behaviour, but Holman Hunt's *Scapegoat* is one of the grim sacrificial images of our culture.

When Sir John Millais painted *Bubbles* he never thought that the Pear's Soap Company would like it as an advert for their product. His image needed no laundering.

Now the innocent, the venal and the laundering come together in a deadly trap, baited with a priceless work of art, and with its jaws set to close not only on Tim but on Sue as well.

JOHN MALCOLM

Sheep, Goats and Soap

The eighth Tim Simpson adventure

THE CRIME CLUB
An Imprint of HarperCollins *Publishers*

The Author asserts the moral right to be identified
as the author of this work.

First published 1991
© John Malcolm 1991

British Library Cataloguing in Publication Data

Malcolm, John
  Sheep, goats and soap: the eighth
  Tim Simpson adventure
  I. Title
823'.914[F]

ISBN 0 00 232339 7

Photoset in Linotron Baskerville by
Rowland Phototypesetting Ltd
Bury St Edmunds, Suffolk
Printed in Great Britain by
HarperCollins Manufacturing, Glasgow

CHAPTER 1

We had no milk left that morning. I had to stump downstairs to see if the new delivery had arrived. I still remember stepping over a jumble of post on the mat to meet a gust of rain as I opened the door. The milk-float was outside and our milkman was limping up the steps, wincing at his much-abused feet clad in a pair of old brown boots that were latticed with creases like wet, collapsed tortoises with sponge rubber stomachs.

''Morning, Ernie,' I said to him, civilly enough. His name isn't Ernie but he rather likes the Benny Hill image it gives him.

''Morning, Mr Simpson.' He relaxed the severe fixity of his working expression, designed to intimidate those motorists who abused his occupation of the through passages in the street. 'Cold, this morning. And wet.' He stamped back down the steps with a rattle of empty bottles and I blessed the fact that although it was a pleasantly domestic anachronism in this part of London still to have a daily milk roundsman, old Ernie had never been much of an early bird.

I addressed myself to the pile of post scattered on the mat and filleted out the first two or three envelopes addressed to me—bills, of course—before I saw another, lying separately. It had been forwarded to me from my old College, something so rare that it came as a shock to realize that they still possessed my address. I slapped the other residents' post on to the hall table and stared at the handwriting. It was familiar but unfamiliar, if you know what I mean: handwriting that you feel you should recognize but which you haven't seen for a long time and you can't put a name to. The postmark was Hastings and that struck a slight chill; I hadn't had a letter from that part of the country within memory but I had been there a few times and rather wished I hadn't, afterwards. The letter whetted my curiosity but I didn't open it until I was back upstairs. It's a sort of ritual in our household that I'm up first to get the breakfast in peace and quiet before the day begins, though why the day only begins when the female element makes its appearance is something I can't explain.

I sat down at the table, opened the milk, poured myself a mug of tea and slit the envelope. The letter was handwritten, rather badly, as though the writer didn't use a pen much these days.

Larks Farm Cottages
Fairlight
Nr Hastings, Sussex.

Dear Tim,

How are you? I can't believe it—I came across an old copy of *Art News* the other day and there you were, grinning like a chimp at some opening, standing by a Monet, a Whistler and an Orpen, of all things. You! You old con-man. Kicking the Oxford front row was the only art you understood when I knew you—how did you do it? I had no idea you'd changed so much. You in art! I couldn't believe it. I told Jane Lardner—you may know her, she's the Vergam Gallery in Hammersmith—that that does it. If a mudsplattered old rugger hack like Tim can make it in art, then so can I. Anyway, I won't go on. I just think it would be a Very Good Thing if we met, soon. It would be worth your while. By all accounts you and your Fund would go big for a couple of paintings I could put your way—very important items. Really. Think of sheep, goats and soap. Geddit?

Seriously, I've a great proposition for you. There's no phone here and I haven't got your address so I'm sending this via the old Coll. It's amazing how they find you—I got an unpaid account the other day!

Are you married yet? I won't be moving round much

and you're welcome to drop in any time—sorry you can't
phone me here.

All the best,
Derek.

I put the letter down and stared out of the window at
the dripping London square outside. The trees in Onslow
Gardens had reluctantly released most of their leaves into
rusty fibrous heaps that cluttered the wet stone pavements
with a soggy, clinging litter. The long panes were tearstained
with spots of rain that spattered insistently on to the dank
surfaces of the city, but I soon lost sight of this as a puzzled
vision of Derek Sedgwick came to mind. Puzzled, because
the letter was uncharacteristically hail-fellow, as though we
had been close pals and as though Derek talked or behaved
in that old-College-chum style: it was quite unlike him.

The last time I had seen Derek had been at a summer-
garden barbecue someone had given in Surrey somewhere—
near Haslemere, that was it—about two years ago; a
business acquaintance who'd been involved in consulting.
Derek had pitched up in filthy khaki shorts and a stained
white Aertex shirt that he must have got from an Oxfam
shop, his beanpole of a figure knobbled like his knees inside
the clothing that hung on him so badly. The Aertex shirt-tail
flapped behind him where it had been half-stuffed into
the Boy Scout's elasticated belt strapping the loose shorts
around him, the S-snake buckle all skewed and the band
twisted over a couple of times where it passed haphazardly
through the belt-flaps on the antiquated shorts. Below the
cobby knees his thin shins went down to soiled feet which
were loosely retained by thonged leather sandals of a size
at least once too big for him. He was a terrible, if endearing
sight. On his arm was an equally grimy girl in a black
sleeveless T-shirt and blue jeans, straight from Portobello
or the Camden Market or somewhere like that, where he'd
obviously picked her up. Everyone gaped in embarrassed
wonder. He'd made a beeline for me, as though we'd been

bosom friends at College instead of the occasional team-mates in scratch rugby sides put together for drinking purposes. Christ, I'd thought then, is that what happens when you let go? At what point, I'd wondered, do you cease to care so completely about your appearance—or is that an appearance in itself?

I picked up the teapot and gave silent thanks that the world inside the flat was more cheerful than the memory of Derek Sedgwick and the grey downpour outside, where the doleful November habit of our tributary of the Old Brompton Road could have had a depressing effect on a man without the uplifting things I was lucky enough to have available.

Sue, for instance. No more cheerful sight could greet the morning than my new wife, smartly turned out in suit, blouse, stockings and shoes, ready for her day at the Tate Gallery, where she works as a Curator. Sue and I had been married at Chelsea Registry Office some months earlier—her first, my second—in the presence of a small but select group of friends who included Sue's mother, my employer Jeremy White of White's Bank and his wife Mary, Chief Inspector Nobby Roberts and his wife Gillian, our Bank accountant Geoffrey Price and his wife, Charles Massenaux of Christerby's and his wife, some ex-College rugby friends of mine and of Nobby Roberts, plus various friends of Sue's from the art world and the Tate. It had been a joyous occasion and some of the ladies had wept copiously, always a good sign at a wedding. Even Nobby Roberts, once the ceremony was over and champagne was fizzing at the restaurant-reception, had taken me to one side and forborne to utter any stern moral warnings as he cocked a glass at me with one hand and leant on his walking-stick with the other.

'Thank heavens for that,' he'd said. 'I do believe we've got you off at last. Was beginning to think it'd never happen.'

'Now, now, Nobby. It was all in Sue's court, as well you know.'

'Yes. Can't think why all these women are so tearful. Gillian was spouting like a burst geyser at the Registry Office.'

'It's the sight of another eligible bachelor lost to them, Nobby. Hearts torn asunder at the view.'

'Ha! Eligible bachelor! You? Some chance. Anyway, I won't go into all that. At least you'll have the incentive to stay out of trouble now.'

'What about you?' I pointed at his walking-stick. 'I hope you'll accept that from now on you're a Whitehall Warrior, or whatever the equivalent in the police force is. A Broadway Bobby? Stick behind a desk and let a constable do the dirty work. Use your brains for a change.'

He drew himself up. Putting down his glass, he moved sideways and leant the walking-stick against a nearby table. Then he stepped back and stood in front of me, arms at his sides. 'How about that? Another month and I'll be throwing the damned thing away for ever.'

'Not bad, Nobby. Not bad at all.' My tone was genuinely respectful. 'I'm impressed.' I was impressed. The injuries Nobby had received months earlier had been horrible, in-flicted on him by a ruthless bunch of criminals. I forbore to dwell on the fact that my old College friend would never play rugby again. Only a man like Nobby, as determined and dedicated as Nobby, would have worked at his own recovery so hard, gone back to work so soon. He looked just like his old self. Only the walking-stick served as a reminder of what he had been through; during the period I had shared in hospital with him I had seen him sweating and wincing in pain as he laboured at a dreadful rehabilitation pro-gramme. It made my own recovery seem ridiculously simple, which it was; far less time was needed for me to be back in form.

'Come on.' I gestured at his glass as I picked up a bottle. 'No backward looks today, Nobby. I want to see you unbuttoning yourself for a bit, d'you hear? This is my wedding, damn it. Drink up. That's an order.'

He had laughed then, and there was a cheer from the others who, I suddenly realized, were watching us. Glasses were raised. Sue and Gillian embraced us tearfully. It was a sort of delayed finale, the last toast to a long series of events that were over, seemed remote, had come to an end. I was married. Sue and I had lived together, of course, before, in this same flat, on and off, but this was serious. We were married at last, and I had made promises to her.

She came and sat at the breakfast table now, giving a rueful glance at the triste scene outside before resting her large blue eyes on me. For some reason I can't explain I had tucked Derek Sedgwick's letter away into my pocket automatically, as though prompted by a subconscious desire to avoid something or at least to ponder on it before taking action. There was something about Derek Sedgwick that, on the few occasions I'd been marginally involved with him, had led to complications, to entanglements, to finding yourself committed to actions or to taking part in scenes that were not normal, that you would never choose given any sort of choice. I remembered an incident after an obscure rugger match at Northampton or somewhere like that, when three of us found ourselves surrounded by police constables while Derek, who had initiated the whole thing, had indeed appeared to be one of us until seconds previously, was nowhere to be seen.

Sue's blue eyes were still on me. 'Hello, husband,' she said.

'	'Morning, wife.'

She poured out some coffee and sipped it before giving a nod of approval. Her gaze wandered over the familiar crockery as I buttered myself some toast.

'How are you, Tim?'

'Fine.' I began to add marmalade. Sue was still looking at me, eyes thoughtful, brown hair smoothly brushed in its waves, clothes crisp and clean. I cut the toast in half. 'Meeting of the Art Fund today.'

'Oh?' Interest came into her voice. 'What about?'

I should perhaps explain that White's Bank have an Art Investment Fund, something Jeremy and I dreamed up to satisfy those clients who wanted to invest in art without actually having to buy a Rembrandt themselves. I am in charge of it, in addition to my other duties, and Jeremy acts as chairman, with Geoffrey Price keeping the accounts. Over a few years we had acquired quite an impressive collection but there had been times when mayhem had intervened, not surprising in view of the attraction the art world has for the forces of anarchy and criminal deceit. The last intervention had had serious results and I was honour bound to avoid anything like it again, now that I was married.

'Nothing much,' I said. 'Just a routine meeting. Review the figures, agree policy, that sort of thing. Chance for Jeremy to participate. See how much we've got to spend on the next acquisition. Decide what it might be.' I bit into my toast and munched on it. 'No surprises.'

'Oh.' Her voice had gone rather flat. 'I see. You don't know what you'll go for next, then?'

'No. We may decide to stay in cash for a bit. Market has been rather hyped lately.'

She nodded thoughtfully. There's something on her mind, I decided, something's bothering her.

'How are things at the Tate?'

'Great.' She brightened. 'There's a lot going on. You know, I told you; the new exhibition.'

'Ah. Yes. Of course.'

She bit her lip. 'Tim?'

'Yes?'

'You are all right, aren't you?'

'Of course. Fit as a fiddle. No problems at all. No after-effects. Doctor says I'm great. I've told you. Those sessions at the gym—'

'No, I didn't mean that. Not physically.' She blushed. 'I know you're all right physically, silly, don't I?'

I grinned at her. 'You mean my mind? Is my mind sound? No, I shouldn't think so. It never was, you know. A Freudian, or perhaps a Jungian, would—'

'No, not that. I don't mean that.' She stopped, cup down in the saucer.

'What, then?' I stared at her, mystified. Was there something wrong with me? Was she regretting something? We had agreed before the wedding that we would go on as before, both of us working, no children yet, she was so keen on her work just then, it was all fine, the only thing was that in view of all the mayhem and the danger of the past, some of which had involved her and some of which hadn't, I was going to lead a normal, quiet, industrious life.

'I'm worried about you.'

'Me? Why?' The mob who had nearly done for Nobby had inflicted a couple of bullet wounds on me, but that was all over. I was fine. She knew that.

She sighed. 'Oh, Tim. You've been so good. Really you have. So quiet.' She refilled her coffee-cup and looked at the breakfast table again. 'That's just it, you see. So quiet. I'm not used to it. It's as though something's knocked the stuffing out of you. You work and you come and go and you still run the Art Fund, very cautiously now of course, and you're OK, you know, you're OK, I mean physically and all that, that's great, and I never want to see you so near death ever again, I decidedly don't, but it's as though something's missing. I mean, I'm not suggesting you get involved in all that—those things that happened before, you know—but—but—'

'But what? You don't think that I should, that I—no, we, because I've promised you and I mean it, I'll never go it alone again—that I should start chasing after things in the art world that could lead to trouble like before? Are you? Those things we did together are part of our old life, Sue. It's all over and done with.'

She nodded and let her troubled eyes look out at the grey,

dripping square. 'I know, I know. I never thought I'd ever say it, never.'

'What? Say what?'

'I miss it, Tim, I really do miss it.'

CHAPTER 2

Women are extraordinary. Incredible. I go to work from
South Kensington Underground Station via the District
Line to Monument and that morning I probably muttered
to myself the whole way. It's not an unusual sight on London
Tube trains of course, seeing even a relatively young man
talking to himself in the morning, but it was unusual for
me. My father would have shaken his head at the sight of
me and made some remark about the effects of modern
living, until he understood the cause. Then he would have
comprehended. You'll never get to understand a woman's
mind, my boy, he used to say, it's impossible. Just when
you think you've got the whole thing wrapped up and
agreed, off they go in the other direction. It really is a
mystery. Don't ask me for advice in that direction, he used
to say, I've never met an expert yet.

I was still somewhat bemused when we assembled for our
mid-morning meeting at the Bank. Jeremy White's office is
not the most resplendent of the Bank's chambers but it is
acceptable enough: mahogany panelled, with a portrait of
Our Founder in his white silk breeches, an oil of a three-
master en route from Manaos to London with a cargo of
the rosewood on which the dynasty was founded and, apart
from Jeremy's handsome Georgian pedestal partners' desk,
a large Cuban mahogany table at which these meetings
are held. Here was Jeremy, tall, blond, in his patrician
mid-forties, and there was Geoffrey Price, the accountant,
married, four children, a house in Hampstead and a Rover
car. We had met often in this way, as Trustees of the Art
Fund, to make our decisions.

Jeremy peered at me genially. 'Hallo, Tim. How are you?'

'Well, thank you, Jeremy. You?'

'Extremely fit. Geoffrey?'

'Thank you, Jeremy. I am well.'

We sat down, assembling our papers. Jeremy peered at me again. 'All right, Tim?'

'Yes, thank you, Jeremy.'

'Um—no—er—after—effects? Fully restored in health and spirits?'

'Yes, thank you. As I have confirmed on several previous occasions.'

'Good, good. Just wondered if, you know, these things can take a bit of time.'

'So I am told.'

'Sue all right?'

'Very chipper, thank you.'

'No problems, then?'

For God's sake, what was the man drivelling on for? How many times did I have to tell him? I raised my eyes from my papers to give him a sharp look and then clouded it with instant remorse. Benevolent concern suffused his whole face. His genial gaze rested on me with kindly welfare, almost anxiety, written large in it. What on earth was the matter? Did I not look well? Was I pale? Surely not; recuperative holidays abroad had given me a reasonable tan, a tan which had not yet faded. A programme of physical exercise, carefully supervised, had restored my whole physical tone. I had never felt better. I had been back at work since shortly after my wedding. Surely it was time for these queries to end? Echoes of my breakfast conversation with Sue came to me. Could Jeremy be barking up the same tree?

Geoffrey Price harrumphed and began his normal peroration. Statement of accounts; valuation of assets, always a delicate matter with art treasures; numbers of contributors; a reference to Christerby's, the fine art auctioneers, in which the Bank has a thirty per cent stake; cash balances.

'Good grief,' Jeremy spluttered. 'How on earth did we come to accumulate so much cash?'

Geoffrey reminded him gently of some previous decisions of his, Jeremy's, and of the disposal of a couple of items of silver and furniture which we had adjudged would remain static in value for a while so the money would be best re-invested elsewhere. The proceeds from these decisions and disposals had now arrived in the accounts. Jeremy stared at me, his expression now totally different.

'For heaven's sake, Tim! We must buy something.'

'The cash,' Geoffrey intervened, 'is earning a good rate on deposit. As I recall, you talked at our last meeting of the market being somewhat hyped up. Of keeping our shots in our lockers, our powder dry, or bilges clean, or something like that. Something quite nautical anyway, I remember, with the object being to conserve cash. You may even have spoken of a war chest.'

Jeremy pursed his lips. Jeremy is a yachtsman and knows very well that his talk is peppered with such references. He ignored these gentle jibes. 'I was referring to the *Impressionist* market, Geoffrey, not the market as a whole. After our last acquisition some caution, some retrenchment, was indicated. Look how right I was: the New York Impressionist sale? Not such high prices, quite a few bought in, unrealized, and that adverse publicity about certain auctioneers lending their clients money to buy Impressionist paintings at auction. Not us, I'm happy to say. Not us.' He paused, waiting for us both to nod in agreement and we obliged, encouraging him to adopt a more ponderous tone. 'There are questions to be asked in that direction, questions of business ethics which we, as a responsible member of the banking and business community, must—'

He broke off because he had caught a glimpse of my face. There is little funnier—or more irritating, depending on your situation—than the spectacle of a merchant banker wittering on about Business Ethics. I was grinning broadly and it brought him up with a sharp explosion.

'Really, Tim! You're an absolute bastard! Really you are!'

'You're not thinking of standing for Parliament, are you, Jeremy?'

'Shut up! To think I was quite worried about you!'

'Why?'

'Never mind that! To business, you wretch! What are we going to do with all that money? Inflation is edging upward again. I don't want to be caught with too much cash about.'

The use of the personal pronoun reminded me of how much Jeremy regarded the Art Fund as his own private hobby. It was Jeremy who energized the Fund forward in a direction which his instincts dictated. It was Jeremy who approved suggestions I might make for investments, filtering them, tailoring them to his own needs, just as he had over the Impressionist acquisition. Both Geoffrey and I were in Jeremy's thrall; he might encourage us, he might be polite, he might even lecture us or veto our votes, all in a spirit of friendly give-and-take, but in the end it was Jeremy who had the major say. Geoffrey often had to act as a brake and even Jeremy knew that there were limits beyond which he could not go, but Jeremy set the pace.

'What about it?' he now demanded. 'I think a large acquisition is called for.'

A call for a large acquisition usually made Geoffrey flinch and adopt an apologetic, querulous tone. Even I was inclined to balk at some of Jeremy's grandiose plans. I opened my mouth to respond but was forestalled.

'If I may contribute.' Geoffrey Price did not sound at all apologetic or querulous. In fact, for him, his tone was surprisingly firm. 'I do not think it would be prudent, no, not at all prudent, to tie up another large sum in one object, as we did with the Impressionist acquisition.' He faced down a peremptory stare from Jeremy. 'Not at all prudent.' A glance came across to me, seeking support. 'In my view the Fund should continue to spread its risk, as it did before.' He held up a restraining hand to check Jeremy, whose mouth had opened. 'I am not saying that the Impressionist acquisition will not yield results. I imply no criticism. But it is a million tied up. Any auditor would be bound to point this out. And I do not think that a responsible Fund Manager would ever ignore the danger of locking too many eggs into one basket. Or should I say filling a basket with one huge egg?' He gave me another glance, more appealing this time. 'Tim?'

When I played the game of rugby I got quite used to having the ball slipped to me by someone who had got himself into a tangle with the opposition, and Jeremy was starting up a pinkish tinge. Generally speaking, the operation of the Art Fund was my pigeon and it was up to me to make sure it prospered. I like Geoffrey Price, always have, and he is just what Jeremy and I need: someone to shove the figures under our noses before we get carried away with our little enthusiasms. It was a time for caution, I felt, perhaps because of previous events, and in my current mood I was prepared to exercise restraint. I nodded approvingly. 'Geoffrey's right, you know, Jeremy. Another one million slab of a purchase is not what we need right now.'

'But the cash, Tim! The cash! Our business is not to retain cash!'

'So we won't. We'll buy, as you want. But not something so grand and international this time.'

Jeremy scowled. 'Something small and parochial, then? Such as?'

'Now, now, Jeremy. You know what our policy has been. We have specialized in items of British art, or British-related art, that represent important steps or are recognized masters in history, especially of the nineteenth century. This has proved successful so far. Perhaps we should continue with this policy.'

His eyes narrowed. He sat back a little. His chin moved up slightly. 'So? What suggestion do you have then?'

It was quite unfair, of course. He and Geoffrey were both staring at me. I mean, to expect a man to come up with an instant suggestion like that, on the spur of the moment, with no prior consideration, no analysis, mere hunch, was quite disgraceful. I felt cornered. We had already been through various episodes with the Camden Town School, the Johns, Whistler, Godwin, Norman Shaw and various worthies of the late nineteenth and early twentieth centuries. It needed calm consideration, this question, not snap judgements. But the City is all about snap judgements, skeet shooting, throws of dice, and Jeremy was waiting. I was unprepared. Perhaps Sue had been right; perhaps in avoiding any probability of danger I had let the stuffing seep out of me to some extent. She and Jeremy both sensed it: something was missing from my demeanour.

'Well?' Jeremy demanded impatiently. 'What about it? Come on, let's have the bright ideas. Seen the light yet?'

And that did it, of course. Came in a flinding blash, as someone said. It hit me like a rocket. Jeremy, mouthing at me, and the letter, suddenly burning away in my pocket. Of course! Sheep, goats and soap! Of course! Soap bubbles, what else? Scapegoats. The clues were obvious.

The light, yet.

The Light of the World. If I'd been superstitious I'd have thought it all an Omen. Definitely an Omen.

'I say, are you all right? Your mouth's wide open, Tim.'

I shut my mouth. I composed myself. I assumed a grave demeanour. I gave them measured looks. Apprehension came into their faces as I addressed them. I was going to enjoy this. They were going to believe I'd thought a lot about this, deeply. Measured tones were called for.

'There is, I regret to say, a major omission in the collection we have assembled to date.' Jeremy's eyebrows shot up: Geoffrey gaped. I got more ponderous. 'It is, I need hardly mention, an omission for which I take the full responsibility. It is an omission which has long taxed my thinking, for which I have long felt a guilt that is perhaps appropriate to the subject-matter. All too appropriate.'

'Tim, for heaven's sake! Cut it out!'

'Jeremy, you of all people must know the omission to which I refer. An omission so glaring that anyone knowledgeable examining the collection that this Art Fund has assembled would be bound to assevereate that its Trustees had ignored a major movement in British Art to the utter detriment of the collection's credibility.'

'Eh? Credibility? Asseverate? What on earth are you drivelling on about?'

'I refer, of course, to a movement in our nineteenth-century art that had a major impact. Indeed, an international impact.'

'What? Impact? In the nineteenth century? Who?'

'The Pre-Raphaelites. Who else?'

I said this with an air of triumph. In my mind's eye there was still an image of Holman Hunt's Christ, with his lantern, his beard and his long robes in the moonlight, knocking on a weed-strewn door that had not opened. *The Light of the World*. A classic Victorian religious painting taken straight from *Revelation*. What was it? *'Behold, I stand at the door and knock; if any man hear my voice and open, I will come in to him and sup with him . . .'* They loved that sort of thing, the Victorians. For them a painting had to have lots of little symbols and a Grand Meaning and a Grave Warning and all that sort of tosh. The Victorians would have given David Hockney's *A Bigger Splash* the raspberry in no uncertain terms, I can tell you. The Victorians took their art seriously. Then there was Holman Hunt's *Scapegoat*, crouched in the suffocating desert with that mauve sky behind, and his sheep on the cliffs or in the cornfield neglected by *The Hireling Shepherd* and then, of course, there was Johnny Millais' *Bubbles*, bought by Pears' Soap and—the whole bang shoot of them. It was a cinch. Sheep, goats and soap. What else?

Jeremy was gaping, a bit like a stranded cod. I decided to help him a little. 'The Pre-Raphaelites, Jeremy. They believed that Raphael and the "Grand Manner" had overdone things. They believed in going back to Truth to Nature, you know. Hence the term: Pre-Raphaelites. Before Raphael—'

He got his jaw working again. 'For heaven's sake! I know what the bloody Pre-Raphaelites were!'

'Ah. Of course. I wondered—'

'Good God! You're not suggesting we buy work by that clown William Morris and that—that—Burne-Jones, are you?'

'No, no, Jeremy. The three original and most important of the Pre-Raphaelite Brotherhood were Rossetti, Hunt and Millais. I was thinking perhaps in terms of Hunt and Millais. Rossetti is a bit hot in price at the moment but Millais was the most successful painter of his time. Technically brilliant. Painted everyone who was anyone. Dozens of 'em. Easily comparable with Sargent but there's no American angle so he doesn't get the prices, yet. He was great. We might buy a first class Millais for a few hundred grand. A Hunt, now—'

'Good grief! I'm not buying *Bubbles* or *Hearts are Trumps*! I can't stand that sort of thing!'

'The Bank is not fond of Continental currencies either, Jeremy, but our Foreign Exchange boys have just made a killing on Dutch guilders and Belgian francs. It's an investment decision, not what you want on the wall. Besides, you know full well we couldn't buy *Bubbles* and—'

'Tim! Really! I do not need a lesson on business! One of the guiding principles, no, one of the most enjoyable aspects of this whole Art Fund affair has been that we all *liked* the things that we bought for it! It wouldn't be fun otherwise! I—'

Geoffrey Price had cleared his throat to interrupt. Jeremy stopped and glared at him.

'What?' he demanded, aggressively.

'I think *Bubbles* and *Hearts are Trumps* are smashing paintings.' Geoffrey was defiant: his jaw jutted forward. 'I think Tim has come up with an absolute winner. An inspired choice. Millais is terrific. *The Black Brunswicker?* Smashing. And Holman Hunt—my God—think of *The Hireling Shepherd* and *The Scapegoat*. They're household names. Superb. Everyone knows them. That was when painting was really painting. None of this contemporary rubbish. What about Ophelia in the stream? No one has ever done anything half as good. The effort those chaps put into a painting makes modern art look ludicrous. Tim's got my vote, let me tell you. One hundred and ten per cent. And no messing.'

Jeremy's eyes were quite round. It was the first time we had ever seen Geoffrey show the slightest enthusiasm for art of any sort. Geoffrey's idea of good investment is bricks and mortar, gilts, blue chips and Government stocks where Governments are of a monetarist hue. But now his face was suffused. His eyes were bright. His waistcoated chest heaved in powerful emotion, straining his gold watch chain. Waves of positive vibration emanated from him, temporarily subduing Jeremy's normal dominance.

'You approve?' he queried of Geoffrey, awestruck. 'You actually approve? You actually believe we should buy a Pre-Raphaelite painting?'

'You bet I do! It's the first time I've ever heard any sense talked at this meeting! In all these years! I mean, I'm not saying the other stuff hasn't done well, of course, there's always a bunch of idiots prepared to believe anything about art and to buy it—but I really do believe that Pre-Raphaelite painting is worth the candle! No one is ever going to turn out that sort of effort again, no one, they haven't got the stamina or the technique nowadays. Bunch of mountebanks, the whole lot of 'em! Art school layabouts. Hunt and Millais turned out paintings you really can admire, every damn professional brush stroke of 'em. None of that blurred half-tone, impressionistic rubbish. Real painting, that was. Subjects you can understand! Every detail dead right! Attaboy, Tim. You go out and get 'em for us. I'm right behind you on this one. Spend all you like! You can forget my previous reservations. This is the big one. Go for it!'

There was an awestruck silence. Jeremy and I stared at him in amazement. I had forgotten that, deep down, despite all the explanations and the so-called art education, what your true-blue Englishman likes is a painting which you can not only understand but in which everything is clearly visible and technically right, so that the wheels on carts could actually turn and the cat's whiskers are placed where a cat's whiskers should be. Detail: they love detail. As for stories: Every Picture Tells a Story should be engraved on the easel of any artist who wants to sell his work in England. It's quite amazing. Poor old Whistler tried to defeat that sort of taste and lost everything he owned in the attempt. It is a taste that runs deep in the nation, still. My Aunt Evangeline used to have Millais prints, *Bubbles* included, and *Hearts are Trumps*, peppered all over her walls. Along with all of Holman Hunt's religious work in steel engravings, or whatever, next to a photograph of Uncle Bertram's grave in the Brompton Cemetery. The PRB struck a chord in the British, no question.

Jeremy had found his voice. He still sounded awestruck. 'Public Taste has spoken,' he said hoarsely, with some malevolence, before making a submissive gesture. 'Who am I to stand in its path! Actually, I suppose I have to concede the—the marketability of that crowd of—of overwrought, sexually frustrated idiots. In Britain, anyway.' He sighed and picked up a pen. 'I take it that it is hereby minuted, apropos of this meeting, that Tim is to proceed to acquire one or more Pre-Raphaelite paintings, subject to the usual approvals on price or prices, at the earliest available opportunity? Do we really have a seconder for that?'

'You certainly have!' Geoffrey was not a bit abashed. 'Hereby seconded. By me. Heartily.'

Jeremy licked his lips. 'Very well. I bow to your judgement. Both of you. I only hope that you know what you are doing. Now, I rather think that it is high time for lunch. More than high time for lunch. My day lies in tatters. What I propose now is a gin and tonic. A very strong gin and tonic. What do you think, Tim?'

'Hereby seconded,' I said, giving Geoffrey a wink. 'A strong gin and tonic, with plenty of bubbles, eh? Bubbles? No, no, don't make me the scapegoat for your anger, Jeremy. Scapegoat? Have you—'

But he was up by that time, striding briskly to the

mahogany cupboard where he keeps his quart of gin. Looking at his back, I started to feel nervous.

We'd never bought anything he disliked before.

CHAPTER 3

Under the first-floor window, the murmur of Old Bond Street was interrupted now and then by the thump of heavy furniture being moved. Occasional voices and calls of warning penetrated the little office above the main rooms of Christerby's, international fine art auctioneers, whose director, or rather one of whose directors, Charles Massenaux, stared at me across the scratched top of his much-abused desk. Shelves of catalogues lined the walls except for the one near his head, where reference books, large and small, made the planking bend under the ponderous content of their pages. His face was set in interest.

'The Pre-Raphaelites?' he echoed. 'You? White's Art Fund?'

Charles Massenaux is a smooth cove. There's no other description for him. He wears the dark pinstripe of the fine art auctioneer along with Jermyn Street shirts and ties that are perhaps slightly too extravagant for, say, a merchant banker. His black shoes are highly polished. His long, pale, well-bred face is topped by thick dark wavy hair which has to be tamped down from time to time by a careful, stroking gesture of the right hand. At the neck this hair curls very slightly upwards in the manner of horse-faced regimental officers who take care that the curl does not extend to the flashiness of someone arty or, say, a Berkeley Square car salesman. These things have to be watched.

'Yes,' I said, keeping it simple. 'The Pre-Raphaelites. Us. I thought, say, a Holman Hunt or a Millais. Or perhaps both. It depends.'

He regarded me carefully. 'Does Jeremy agree with this?'

I hesitated just a fraction. 'It was a unanimous decision of the Trustees. The Fund lacks balance without such an acquisition.'

The hint of a sardonic smile came to Charles Massenaux's face. 'I bet Jeremy argued like hell. He hates the Pre-Raphaelites.'

'Jeremy is not fond of William Morris. Or Burne-Jones. But they were later additions to the Brotherhood. If it could still be called that.'

'Burne-Jones—' Charles Massenaux tilted his chair back with a fond, reminiscent smile as he launched into an imitation of the peremptory tones of Jeremy in an irascible mood. I knew what he was going to say and I joined in chorus with him.

'*Burne-Jones? Burne-Jones? Man painted as though he'd never seen a pair of buttocks in his life!*'

We burst out laughing. Charles Massenaux's manner broke and he grinned at me like a Cheshire Cat. 'Have some coffee, Tim?'

'Great.'

'I do enjoy these little visits of yours. Much better than your attendance at our board meetings.'

'Thank you. I take it that that is meant as a compliment.'

His grin became sly as he called for the coffee. Due to White's share ownership in Christerby's, I had been appointed as a non-executive director to keep an eye on things. Those attendances were more serious affairs and no one was likely to come out at them with Jeremy's favourite quotation on Burne-Jones, culled from Aldous Huxley's novel *Point Counterpoint* in which Bidlake, the Augustus John Bohemian artist-figure, makes the unflattering comment. Charles Massenaux is Christerby's director particularly concerned with nineteenth- and twentieth-century painting, a wizard on the Impressionists, something he shares with Sue. I have often chatted to him about an acquisition or likely acquisition before taking the plunge, which is why he was at our wedding: Charles is an old friend.

'Rossetti?' he queried, cocking a dark eyebrow at me. 'Is there any reason why you have omitted Rossetti? Quite

apart from Jeremy's prejudices, of course. Is there a prejudice of your own, perhaps?'

'Ah.' I didn't want to admit, just then, that I have never
really liked Rossetti. To me Rossetti is too, I don't know,
equivocal a figure. Without Rossetti the Brotherhood would
not have existed, but then what was the Brotherhood anyway? Hunt and Millais soon forgot it. And Rossetti, to my
knowledge, had little to do with sheep, goats or soap, which
was another good reason.

Charles was still watching me. I cleared my throat. 'I
thought—I got the impression—that Rossetti might be a
bit too hot for us.'

'Mmmm.' He reached for his coffee.

'I don't know why I thought that. I just did.' I reached
for mine.

He abandoned his cup and put the tips of his fingers
together, arch-like. His eyes rested on me thoughtfully. 'You
are extraordinary, Tim. Really you are.'

'Me? Why?'

'Well, I suppose because you're right, in a way.' The tips
of his fingers remained together. 'You see, there are two
major directions, two major schools of Pre-Raphaelitism if
you look at it from a cold-blooded, mercenary point of view.
Our view, I suppose. First there is the romantic direction,
the misty sort of subject-matter headed by Rossetti and
Burne-Jones. Romantic ladies like Proserpine and knights
in armour from Malory. Right now those are the in thing.
Pop stars and the music world particularly go for them. Big
money.'

'Really?'

'Oh yes. The collections of certain famous figures in
the popular musical world are examples which spring to
mind.'

'Good grief. It's a good job I didn't try to steer Jeremy
in that direction, then. Anyone else?'

'Oh yes. Quite a few. And, of course, the Japanese.'

'Eh?'

'The Japanese. They have rather a lot of knights in armour in their own history. That sort of thing appeals to them enormously. There's always big Japanese money for a Malory subject. Of course, Burne-Jones is not always thought of as a Pre-Raphaelite, having joined later, so to speak, but he did a lot of that knightly stuff and has to be included. It's difficult—later and other parts of the movement like Arthur Hughes and William Dyce fetch big money too, about eight hundred thousand or so. Then there's the elder statesman and father-confessor, Ford Madox Brown.'

'Hang on. You're going too fast. What was, or is, the other major direction?'

'Ah, this is the interesting part. The Hunt and Millais part, which you have lighted upon. It's the Truth to Nature part. Not as popular, which may be a good reason to invest in it, you know. I'm sure I don't have to tell you that religious subjects tend to be difficult to sell and Holman Hunt's major series was religious. He did paint other things but he took ages to complete a picture. Ages. He was terribly painstaking. An early Hunt would be terribly rare. Might cost you a million.'

'A million? Good grief. What about Millais?'

'Ah, Johnny Millais. There's a story for you. The most successful and the wealthiest painter of his day. Handsome. Rich. Portraits, of course. And pretty girls, little girls especially. Soldiers saying farewell to their sweethearts before going off to be killed. Tear-jerkers. *Bubbles*. *Hearts are Trumps*. Didn't drink, like Orpen, and was happily married, unlike Sargent. Almost too good to be true, Millais.'

'So?'

'So I'm rambling. Millais is technically brilliant. I mean, *Ophelia* is the classic Truth to Nature painting. There are fifty-seven varieties of plants and flowers in that painting, every single one of them with some vital significance or another to the subject-matter. All depicted perfectly. He did quite a few watercolour copies of it for various people and

SHEEP, GOATS AND SOAP 29

even one of those would set you back fifty grand or more. One of the great images of our culture. Even one of his pretty children of no consequence sold for two hundred thousand the other day. He didn't half turn it out, mind. There must be portraits all over the place. The Boy Wonder. Darling of the Academy.'

'Do I sense a certain dislike in your tone, Charles?'

He sighed. 'I suppose you do. Actually, it's probably because I've been programmed to believe that all that sort of painting is crap. I'm brainwashed by Impressionism, you see.'

'Whistler was the same. He thought that Victorian subject-painting was terrible.'

'I know. And look what happened to Whistler. The Great British Public gave him the bird. A big raspberry. There must still be an enormous following for Millais. You're probably on to a good thing.'

'Well, don't sound so depressed about it. After all, Impressionism has proved to be the winner, not the Pre-Raphaelite Brotherhood, as far as modern opinion, taste and money go.' I stood up. 'Thanks for the coffee, Charles. And the advice. Two hundred thousand is nothing to pay for a painting these days.'

'You wouldn't get a major one for that.'

'No. But it means there may be a chance of getting something at a reasonable price. Thanks.'

He nodded. 'Glad to help. Nice to see you, Tim, as usual. You look well. You've been very quiet lately, I must say. Married life suiting you?'

'Oh yes.'

'Give Sue my best. Great girl.'

'Yes, I will.'

His eye caught mine. 'Keeping out of trouble too, I suppose?'

'Of course.'

'Bit dull, eh? Still, I can't see a Millais bringing the Mafia down on your head, somehow.'

'No, no. Piece of cake. You can rest assured, Charles, that the mayhem is off for the duration.'

He put a finger to his lips. 'Ssh. The gods may hear you. As they so often have before.'

CHAPTER 4

The road to Hastings hadn't improved much since I'd last chased down it. You still have to untangle yourself from the sprawl of South-East London and then flank Sevenoaks and Tonbridge to where the road narrows back before the clever Pembury by-pass which has moved the bottleneck to a point north of the village. After that the road is the same winding country lane disguised as an A category so that gypsum lorries and great loads of spun concrete sewage pipes from Rye can crawl up the hills.

When the first oast houses poked their conical, steepled roofs over the hedges Sue began to relax and to hum softly to herself. The Jaguar burbled its way easily along; there was no great hurry and an early Saturday morning in November does not produce the great trek to the coast that easier seasons initiate. It had stopped raining, though, and was one of those clear, blowy days that bring out ramblers in khaki anoraks and boots, people clutching binoculars for birdwatching.

'How do you know he'll be there?' Sue asked suddenly, taking her eyes off a cock pheasant that was stalking suicidally along the grass verge beside the road.

'Oh, he'll be there. I sent him a note, since he's got no phone, and he did say that he wasn't going anywhere. I expect he's stony broke, as usual. He always was and I don't think those paintings of his command a lucrative following, if he's still churning them out. His domestic economy has always been a mystery. I think his girlfriends bail him out.'

Sue gave me a rather prim look and turned back to the window. 'He doesn't sound a very attractive character.'

I thought of Derek Sedgwick, thin and unkempt, always pursuing the chimera of artistic wealth, trying to promote his latest work, work always tailored to what he thought might be the fashionable trend, bending to every breeze, knowledgeable but hopeless, enthusiastic but fatalistic, his bright eye engaging every nuance of expression in the hope that his current interlocutor might provide a break, a hint, an opportunity for making gain. Thinking back of him as I had known him at College, where he had most inappropriately read economics, I realized now that he really belonged to a bygone era, when an undergraduate might not have to work, when the terms could be spent as Derek had spent them, talking, drinking coffee, listening to jazz, joining æsthetic societies in order to meet girls, dishevelled, chukka-booted, self-indulgent and amoral, the sort of student our present, grim-visaged, economic-reality era does not encourage in any sense.

'I think you'll rather like Derek. He's an awful example to us all. He's a mountebank and a charlatan and all that, he can't paint for toffee and he talks sheer rubbish. Society needs people like Derek. Not just for necessary comparison purposes but because he can be very appealing and he's not stupid. He's the spectre following us all. He's always sussed out every nook of the art market and knows exactly what's needed about a month after it's all happened. Derek is the exact opposite of Sunday supplement society. Totally unsuccessful yet often so near to a breakthrough. He did a promotion about six years back when he filled a gallery with his latest work and sold the lot. He actually collected about half of the money too, about eight thousand, I believe, but lost the rest.'

'Lost it? How?'

'Oh, he was greedy, you see, and believed some New York crook who took the other half of the work saying he'd get double the price for it in the States and then never paid up. The usual story. Derek spent the money he did collect on a disused stable on the Spanish side of the Pyrenees near Pamplona or somewhere like that. It was going to be a studio but it's probably fallen down by now.'

Sue shook her head gently. 'Did he have any training as a painter?'

'Oh no. Formal training would only inhibit an artist like Derek. Actually, he never showed any interest in painting at Cambridge. I think it was a girl he lived with in Fulham who got him into that. Something to do with faking Art Deco linocuts. You know, 'thirties stuff.'

Sue's lips pursed and she frowned. The trouble with being a serious professional in the art world, like Sue, is that the massive fringes of that society can be an intense embarrassment, like poor junk food to a three-star chef. Sue shifted in her seat and noted the last road sign to Hastings.

'Well,' she said, 'I hope he's not wasting your time, Tim.'

'You never know with Derek. He's always wanted to deal on the side. He sold some very good sketches of Paul Nash's not so long ago. The reference to Hunt and Millais was obvious. Sheep, goats and soap. What else could that be?'

'Nothing that I know of. And, of course, the area is spot on.'

'Eh?'

'The area. Hastings. Particularly Fairlight.'

'Really? I seem to remember that Rossetti and Lizzie Siddal were married in Hastings because she was always being sent there for her health, but you've lost me on Hunt and Millais. I don't suppose it's anything more than coincidental, whatever the association is. What is it, by the way?'

She smiled indulgently. 'Holman Hunt's painting of sheep was done on the cliffs at Fairlight. He stayed with Edward Lear while sketching it out. Not *The Hireling Shepherd*. I'm talking of the painting called *Our English Coasts* or *Strayed Sheep*. It's Hunt's most celebrated landscape—Delacroix raved about it—I don't see it every day, Tim, but certainly at least once or twice a week. If not more often.'

'In the Tate?'

'In the Tate.' Sue nodded emphatically. 'Along with *The Awakening Conscience*. Very moral. All sorts of lessons for us all, there are, in those two paintings. Sheep exposed on the edge of cliffs—there's a black one, leading the others to destruction—and a girl having Second Thoughts about misbehaving with a smoothie.'

'Hum. Er, yes. What about Millais?'

'*The Blind Girl*. That's in Birmingham, now. He went for a walk with Hunt and Lear along the coast from Fairlight to Rye. Must have passed Winchelsea on the way because it's the village on the hill in the background to *The Blind Girl*. About six or seven miles from Fairlight? The girl is Effie, of course. Ruskin's ex-wife.'

'Good heavens. I had no idea the place was so thick with Pre-Raphaelites. No wonder Derek has latched on to them. I say, won't it be exciting if he really has turned up something unknown, something very good?'

Sue grinned and put her hand on my knee. 'Tim, you really are just a boy at heart. Do you know that you've quite changed? Back to your old self? You love a treasure hunt, don't you? So do I, I admit it, but it's life-blood to you. Look at you: your eyes are shining.'

'Well—' I slowed down, we were coming to the outskirts of the town—'I'm not sure that I admit to all that. But the Art Fund has always been a bit of a treasure hunt. Jeremy and I started it for that reason; for a bit of fun. So, in a sense, you're right.'

'Of course I am. And I'm glad. I've been quite worried about you.'

She turned back to look at the passing grounds of large houses as I turned off the main road to the east and followed the high ridge above the town. After some winding about we came down to the Winchelsea road behind the town at an area called Clive Vale, where the signposts indicated the route to Fairlight.

'Clive Vale Farm,' Sue said, half to herself, 'that's where Lear and Holman Hunt stayed.'

I grinned at her this time. 'My bloodhound,' I said. 'I thought you were an Impressionist freak? No time for the Pre-Raphaelites.'

'My tastes are irrelevant. No serious art historian in England can afford to ignore Hunt, Millais and Rossetti.'

The road curved up away from the town on to pastured headlands above the sea, which was invisible but somehow present to our right.

'I need some petrol,' I said. 'I'll get directions to Lark's Farm at the nearest garage.'

A small filling station came up on our left. Down here the wind was blowing much stronger and the garage signs flapped or rotated at dangerously high revs. A few clouds streamed rapidly across a much colder sky than London had provided. It was a self-service place and my jacket wasn't nearly thick enough for the penetrating wind, making me hunch and huddle as I squeezed the fuel pistol trigger hard to get the fill over with as quickly as possible. Sue remained, warm and relaxed, inside the car. The forecourt was wet and dirty, as though grimy rain had sluiced it down. Two or three cars of unattractive appearance were marked with similarly unattractive second-hand prices. An old, pale greyish-blue Morris Minor 1000 of well-worn appearance was parked down the side-alley leading to a workshop door. Used tyres and oil drums were piled against flaking plant walls. It reminded me of the homespun garages of ten years ago or more, before the big chains took over and introduced bright plastic cladding to roadside décor. This was a survival, uneconomic and unsuccessful, doubtless dismissed as a prospect by the big oil companies.

The wind was cutting; it was a relief to get inside the pay cabin even though it was thick with cigarette smoke. An aged attendant coughed behind a roll-your-own fag end and remained seated, unblinking, at a dirty counter stacked with peanuts and cans of oil.

'Lark's Farm,' I said to him, as he handed me the credit card slip to sign. 'Is that near here?'

'It is. Half a mile down the way you're going, on the right. There's a lane leads to it.'

'The cottages must be close to it, I suppose? Lark's Farm Cottages?'

The old man bared his teeth in a yellow, stained smile. 'If they're still there, they will be, aye.'

I frowned, perplexed. 'Still there?'

The old man smiled wider. 'Half of Lark's Farm has gone into the bloody sea, mate. Over the last few years. Cottages are condemned. Right on the edge, they are.'

'Edge?'

'Sure. Edge. Of the cliffs. Bloody cock-up somewhere down the Channel. Built a great pier. Altered the current. Coast from Fairlight right along to Pett Level went in nearly six feet last year. Council says it's safe now but I wouldn't fancy it.'

'Six feet? Six feet? That's a hell of a lot!'

'It is, certainly is. Whole of Gracker's Fields—used to walk my dog across 'em—all fallen in over the years. The whole bloody lot. Gardens all round the cove, too. Most of Lark's Farm, well, it's not really a farm any more. Smallholding, more like. Camping site. Cliff edge is dangerous, I can tell you. Path keeps going over.'

'Good grief. A friend of mine is supposed to live in Lark's Farm Cottages. You say they're condemned?'

A look of suspicion crossed the old man's face. 'A friend? Who'd that be?'

'Sedgwick. Derek Sedgwick.'

He glared down at the credit card slip and then gave a quick glance up towards the Morris Minor in the alleyway. 'Mr Sedgwick, eh?' His eyes narrowed. 'Did I note your licence number? On the slip?'

'I'm sure I don't know.'

He shoved a greasy ballpoint pen at me. 'Put down your number. On the slip.'

Miserable old fool; couldn't even use the word please.

'Put it down yourself.'

His eyes widened and his jaw slackened. I wrenched open the door, allowing a gust of stale blue vapour to stream out into the wind.

'Here!' he called indignantly.

I stumped across the garage yard, clutching at my jacket to close it. Inside the car it was warm and cosy, partly scented by Sue. I caught a glimpse of the old man's face through the dirty kiosk window; he was angrily writing down my licence number as I drove back on to the road.

'Miserable old bugger.'

Sue's eyebrows raised themselves in amusement. 'Having trouble with the natives? Wouldn't he tell you where it is?'

'Only too graphically. The coast is falling into the sea along here, apparently. And he's obviously been exposed to Derek Sedgwick's particular brand of credit extension.'

Sue frowned in puzzlement. 'The coast? What has that to do with it?'

'The cottages are near the edge. They're supposed to be condemned. Knowing Derek, he's probably taken one at a peppercorn rent because no one else will live there.'

'Good heavens.' She fell silent, leaving me with a distinct sense of unspoken criticism about the habits, habitat and honesty of my acquaintance. Fortunately the lane mentioned by the old lag at the garage came up fairly quickly on our right and I turned into it, wincing at an initial shower of loose stones that peppered the underside of the car with a staccato spatter of paint-chipping flints. I slowed to a crawl as the lane, losing its gravel surface, narrowed into a track with a weedy green centre and hedges to either side. It continued steeply up, approaching the headland by the sea towards a lightening sky, giving the impression that it would suddenly disappear into the wide white yonder, aerial-bound. Sheep on the rather sparse, springy green fields beside us stared curiously with their bulging dark eyes as we bumped past. Wind ruffled the scrub beside the field railings and moaned against the car window. We passed a blue notice, very tattered, that said 'POLICE. DANGER. KEEP

OUT' and I assumed this was a warning to keep clear of the cliff edges at the end of the track.

'I read an article in *Country Life* once,' Sue said, suddenly, 'that I'm sure worked out that Holman Hunt painted his scene from somewhere around here. I remember now: they said that it's fallen into the sea. The place where he painted, I mean; there must be a lot of erosion about.'

'That's what the old fool at the garage said. Oops!'

I managed to brake quickly before running into the back of a parked car, left inconsiderately just round a turn that blocked the view ahead. Fortunately the bumpiness of the track had reduced my speed to a crawl in deference to the springs on the Jaguar, so I pulled up fairly short. The vehicle was a dark Ford Escort with no one in it. In turn, it had stopped behind a fire-engine.

'A fire-engine!' Sue's voice was incredulous. 'What on earth is a fire-engine doing here?'

I didn't hear any more. I was out of the car, into what was now almost a gale that blew my tie off my shirt and round my neck. I buttoned my coat as I strode quickly up past the big red vehicle. A row of brick cottages met my sharp stare into the freezing wind, at least most of a row of brick cottages of the kind that go with farms, those small terraced dwellings, usually two down and three up, that have an earth privy at the back of a yard and small front gardens with hollyhocks and turnips growing promiscuously together.

The end of this terrace was missing.

There was a shattered, blown-out look to it, with splintered beams and jagged brick edges and rag-ends of slates that looked like a wartime photograph of the East End of London during the bombing. Beyond this ragged smash-end was nothing; a huge gap with a dizzy view of the sea booming up the coast to a point far below my eye level, out of sight. On either side of the terrace the sparse green grass raced up to the cliff edge, swirling round the terrace-block of cottages in a surge of meadow that seemed to have a sloping impulse to propel everything overboard. Moving cautiously round the broken end of the terrace were figures in fireman's uniform, some with helmets, and one or two in civilian dress. The icy cold wind intensified as I strode towards the cottages, throwing some spatters of rain or spray at me. As I got closer I could see that a huge fresh chunk of cliff had broken away; new earth marked a great bite out of the edge in a semi-circular pattern that curved round to embrace the terrace, taking the end of it off in a shearing action. Some of the figures were peering very cautiously over the fresh edge, holding ropes.

'Hey!' One of the civilian figures shouted at me. 'Get back, there! Back! It's very dangerous!'

I paid no attention. Shock numbs the reception of certain messages and I was up to the nearest fireman before the civilian began to scramble towards me. The fireman was a big fellow, encased in thick blue serge, great boots and a helmet. An axe was strapped to his waist. He held up a large hand.

'Hold hard there, sir,' he boomed. 'No further. It's very dangerous; the whole edge is completely unstable. Stay where you are.'

I pulled up short before him, peering into his weather-beaten face. 'Is everyone all right?'

He shook his head.

'No, sir, I'm afraid everybody is not all right. It all went down in the night. They think there's some poor fellow gone down with the cliff. Possibly more than one person, they say. It's a dreadful business. Wasn't supposed to be anyone in these cottages, even though the Council did put out that the cliffs are all right here now.'

'Jesus Christ.' I glanced back towards the Jaguar. Sue was getting out, winding a headscarf round her hair. The civilian who had shouted at me was capering officiously back from the edge towards me, his jacket straining at the centre button where the wind was drawing it taut around him. I had a giddy look downwards beyond the end of the

ragged brickwork towards the booming sea in the distance.
Between the cliffs and the singing waves two hundred feet
below there was a steep, receding tangle of boulder-like
lumps of broken land, half covered with a mixture of grass,
gorse, dense brambles and clay. It was an untidy cascade,
an unattractive result of collapse and erosion, of movement
outwards. Nearer at hand was a fresh, ugly pile of great
slices of sod, bricks, splintered timber, plastered internal
walling, even patterned wallpaper, all in a heap well below
us and, apart from this central heap, material was scattered
sideways and downwards beyond. I didn't feel at all safe. It
came to me that anyone living in these cottages must have
been particularly unaffected by heights and instability or
just plain desperate for a roof over his head. It was an
amazing view to look out on but it was a condemned
view, the view of someone either short-term in thinking or
mentally abnormal. Sue was starting towards me and I
turned to ward her off from the danger of the edge just as
the capering civilian came up, all rigid features, officious
movements, upward set to the head.

'Oy!'

I ignored him, moving forward to prevent Sue from
progressing further. 'Tim! How dreadful! When did this
happen?'

'Last night, apparently. There's someone in it. I'm afraid
it must be Derek. No one else would be living—'

'Here!' The suited man was about the same age as me,
darkish, insinuating. He seemed to think he had right of
way in the place but he was a bit puffed as well as wind-
blown. 'Keep back! It's dangerous here. Unauthorized per-
sonnel are not permitted. We're about to cordon the area
off; I must ask you to leave. Didn't you see the notice back
there? Eh?'

I looked at him irritably. Concern about Derek Sedgwick
was making me jumpy. I glanced at him, feeling the stirring
of some previous familiarity, a past memory, flit through
my mind as we faced each other. His features were known

to me and I saw him frown in concentration for a moment before his face cleared and a not altogether friendly expression came across it.

'Well, well,' he hooted, above the howl of the wind. 'Look what the gale's blown in. I don't believe it. I never forget a face. Especially when its owner tried to bash me the last time we met. Simpson, isn't it? *Mister* Tim Simpson, our superior officer Roberts's mate?'

'Yes, I'm Simpson.'

'And what are you doing here, might I ask?'

The question took me aback. I was about to give him a sharp retort when I looked into his face. It was creased, lined anxiously, irritably, as though I had intruded upon more than this dreadful disaster. I looked closer to try and clarify the reason, just as clarification dawned.

'Good heavens.' I remembered now. 'Foster. Sergeant Foster, of Hastings CID. What a small world.'

'Inspector Foster now, Mister Simpson.' He moved closer to me, still not in a friendly way. 'You haven't answered my question.'

I stared at him. I had not seen Foster since a rather angry exchange in an antique shop on Hastings seafront three years before. If it hadn't been for Nobby's restraining presence then, I might easily have dotted him one. So now he was an inspector. He had placed himself close to me, too close for pleasantry. I scowled at him.

'You still in the CID?'

'I am.'

'CID cover accidents now, do they? Thought you were only interested in crime. Or do you double as a fireman as well?'

His face puckered. 'That's my business. Are you acquainted with this man Sedgwick?'

'Yes, I am. Is he all right? I mean, was he in the house when it went over?'

'That is what we are trying to establish. If we aren't hindered with our work. How well do you know him?'

His manner was hardly reassuring. It seemed to me that this was not the time for this line of talk. 'I am acquainted with him. Why? What's it to you?'

'Tim.' Sue's voice, breaking in, carried a note of warning. She moved close to me.

Foster pushed his face towards mine. 'I'll tell you what it is to me, although I don't have to. What it is to me is the interest I take in people who are in the habit of pushing up their noses things that they shouldn't be pushing up their noses. That's what it is to me. So now maybe you'd like to be a little more explicit about your acquaintanceship with Sedgwick, would you? Perhaps you'd like to make a statement about that, would you?'

Hackles started up on the back of my neck. 'Here? Now? On what grounds?'

'On the grounds of making a statement.' His voice rose. 'A statement assisting the police with their inquiries. Into the sniffing activities of—'

'Now see here, Foster—' I took a sharp step forward.

'Tim!' Sue grabbed my arm.

Foster leaped back a foot, a full hop of alarm. 'Oy! Don't you threaten me! I'll not have any of that!'

The big fireman nearby grinned broadly, upsetting Foster further. He shoved a finger at me. 'None of that!'

'You bloody insinuate we're involved in sniffing drugs, Foster, and I'll pitch you over the edge along with the rest of the rubbish!'

His voice rose. 'Don't you threaten me! I didn't insinuate!'

'Oh yes you did!'

'Oh no I didn't!'

'Tim! Inspector! Really! Like two little boys!'

Foster blinked at Sue resentfully. 'The activities of Sedgwick are a legitimate concern of our inquiries. I did not infer that you were involved in drug-taking. I am perfectly entitled to investigate this very serious incident! Anyone who knows—or knew—Sedgwick, who was residing—I should say squatting—here, should be glad to assist us!'

It was incredible. Here we were on the edge of a beetling cliff, the wind howling round us, clouds scudding just above, the terrace looking like something the Luftwaffe had just had a go at, firemen heaving on ropes, Derek Sedgwick probably lying crushed to pulp in the wreckage below, and his pompous ass was behaving like a village constable at a burgled sweetshop.

'Oh come on,' I said, heavy with sarcasm. 'The CID? At a collapsed cliff? What will you be insinuating next? That he stuffed a load of dope up his nose and sneezed so hard it brought the cliff down? Good God man, you must be desperate.' I waved my hand at the shattered terrace. 'You'll be saying next that someone stuck a charge of dynamite under the cliff and blew the whole bloody lot off, noses, sniffers, Derek and all.'

Foster blinked at me. His face took on a curious look, curious and surprised simultaneously. He looked into my face with real astonishment. Opening his mouth, he turned to gesticulate towards the edge but was interrupted by the big fireman, whose grin had disappeared.

'You'd better come along,' he called to Foster, pitching his voice above the wind. 'We've found a body. Right under the heap below.'

CHAPTER 5

It was much warmer back inside the car, out of the wind. Sue was shivering visibly and I started the engine, turning the heater on high to blow warm air across us. In front of us the dark blue Escort—presumably Foster's—and the fire-engine stood in metallic silence. The hedge to our right heaved and ruffled in the weather. Somewhere down on the edge, Foster and the firemen were still conferring, doubtless peering over at men working in the wreckage below. I felt shocked. There was a dreadful numbness to me, like someone who has lost something he's not quite sure of and isn't really convinced he's lost it. It was as though a computer had wiped something from a memory, something that you'd worked on and reserved and now it wouldn't bring back again. You knew it was there, or had been, and you wanted it back. A gap, that's what it was.

'Exposed sort of place,' I said, more to break the silence than anything else and hoping that some sort of banality would assuage our ghastly thoughts. 'I don't see this as Derek's style at all. He was never the one for a bracing climate when I knew him. If I did know him. He wasn't one to sniff things, either. Didn't even drink much. Didn't like losing control.'

'Hastings,' Sue said, getting her teeth to stop chattering and her mouth to work. 'Low cost. Read any artistic biography and you'll find someone who failed and had to retreat to Hastings to live. Jack Knewstub, after the affair at the Chenil Gallery with the Johns. Whistler's mother. Edward Lear. Banting. He—Derek Sedgwick—was here to save money. From what you say.'

'Bit of a drastic economy, Sue. No one in his right mind would choose to save money by living on the edge of disaster like that. Literally on the edge. I know that people hang on to their houses to the bitter end but that was ridiculous.'

A fireman clumped up to the engine, heaved himself into the cab and started up the vehicle's motor. A cloud of diesel smoke puffed from its exhaust and was whipped away by the wind. The fire-engine heaved, jerked, then moved slowly up the track, turning off it on to the grass. It lumbered forward cautiously, down towards the cottages, passing out of sight beyond the hedge. Inspector Foster appeared around the corner of the same hedge, stared briefly at us, and then got into the Escort. I saw him pick up a mike and start talking into it.

'I think we are a little *de trop*,' I said, doing up my seat-belt. 'My feeling is that we should retire from the scene with as much dignity as we can muster. It's going to be a while before anyone makes any statements about anything or even tells us anything and, frankly, I don't want to be present when they pull Derek's somewhat damaged remains out of that morass of broken masonry, etcetera. Not present at all. I think we've had quite enough excitement for one morning.'

Sue turned to look at me. I swallowed nervously. There's a thing Sue has about me and trouble and its avoidance. In the past it has led to differences, severe differences, and tiffs of one sort or another, some of them very distressing and long drawn out. I didn't want all that to rear up again. I mean, it wasn't as though I'd gone looking for this, now had I? If Derek Sedgwick had been crazy enough to live in a condemned cottage on the edge of a crumbling cliff it was his affair, not mine. It was just a matter of unfortunate timing, really, that the previous night's gale had finally tipped the scale. I couldn't help it, could I?

Sue put her hand on my arm. It was as though she'd been reading my thoughts. 'It's your old problem with timing again, Tim.' Her voice was soft, sympathetic. 'Poor old Tim. You just can't help it, can you, my sweetheart? It seems incredible. I mean, I didn't know Derek Sedgwick and I have a feeling that I probably wouldn't have liked

him, but I'm desperately sorry about what's happened. For
you, too. I know he didn't mean that much to you, but there
was the possibility of the Pre-Raphaelites and everything.'
She leant across and kissed me, gently. 'Just when you turn
up, bang goes the man, clean over a cliff.' She bit her lip
and shook her head. 'It's extraordinary. I wouldn't have
believed it possible. And I egged you on to this. I know I
did. At breakfast the other morning. I want you to know
I'm with you, Tim, whatever happens. I'm your wife now
and I feel much more responsible. I can see what makes
you tick, well, I've always known what made you tick but
I didn't want to admit it.' She looked across at me. 'You
mustn't give up. You'll have to see if you can find those Pre-
Raphaelites some other way.'

'I know. And thanks, Sue. All I can hope is that he didn't
have them in the cottage with him.'

She frowned a little, but smiling. 'Trust you to say that.
I can't imagine, though, that anything really valuable would
be kept there.'

'No.' I put the car into reverse and turned round to look
back down the lane. 'I don't think so, either.'

Foster's face appeared at my window. He must have
nipped out of his car the moment he saw the movement of
the Jaguar.

'Where are you going?'

I motored the window down. 'What?'

'I said where are you going?'

'Home, Inspector. We are going home. There is nothing
further we can contribute to this appalling scene and you
have made it abundantly clear that we are *non grata*. We
have no place here.'

Foster regarded me steadily. Then he nodded abruptly.
'All right. If we need to get in touch with you, we will.'

I bowed my head courteously. 'Simpson. Onslow Gardens. We're in the telephone book.'

His mouth gave a qurikish twist and then straightened
itself. 'I think we can manage to find you,' he said. 'And

it's well you're leaving. This place will be clogged with forensic and all sorts within minutes. We don't need any public here.'

'Goodbye then, Inspector. We'll phone to find out what's happened.'

'Goodbye, sir. Madam.' There seemed to be no irony in his voice. His face had gone impassive. I reversed steadily down the track, ricking my neck to get a proper view backwards. At the stony end my wheels spun once before we regained the road. With relief I drove on to the firm surface and turned back the way we had come. The car went into forward drive and eased thoughtfully down the tarmacked way towards Clive Vale. It had been both a shock and a disappointment. Characters like Derek Sedgwick are like the signposts of life; you may not like the messages but you feel a sense of loss without them. I could visualize Jeremy's and Geoffrey's faces at our next meeting, when I would have both much and little to report. I'd been cocky about our next investment; this was another lesson to me. I'd have to slog the usual routes now, auction houses and dealers and God knew what. All I'd done was to give Sue another demonstration of my capacity to discover disasters; despite the affectionate way she'd taken it I felt it was a poor business, a business I should not have experienced. I was upset.

The dingy garage came up on my right, its lurid notices rotating and flapping. The gaggle of poor-quality second-hand cars still forlornly awaited their undiscriminating buyers but the Morris Minor in front of the workshop had gone.

The old, faded, pale grey-blue Morris Minor wasn't there.

I pulled in to the side of the road so sharply that a following pickup nearly rammed me. It hauled past, hooting loudly.

'Tim! What on earth?'

Into my mind's eye there came first that miserable old

garage codger, glancing out instinctively towards the Minor when Derek Sedgwick's name was mentioned. Then, from farther back, dredged from memory came a view of Derek in filthy old Aertex Oxfam shirt and worse khaki shorts, beanpoling into that Haslemere garden-party with his grimy Camden Lock girl. Behind him, in that memory-flicker, I could see a pale rusted Morris Minor parked in the driveway among the Rovers and Volvos and Jaguars. Derek had owned that old Morris Minor for years.

'That was Derek's Minor,' I said out loud, sitting in my stationary car.

'What?' Sue was flustered, concerned. 'Tim, what are you talking about? What Minor?'

I jerked my thumb back at the garage. 'The Morris Minor that was parked in the alleyway beside the filling station, in front of the workshops. That was Derek's Minor. Probably in for repairs or something. Probably couldn't pay for it. It's gone now. I mean, since we were there.'

She gave me a long, wide-eyed look for a moment and then burst out laughing, not even hysterically. 'Tim, really! You're hopeless! Hopeless! There's no changing you, is there? Why should it be Derek's? There are thousands of Morris Minors about, still. Lots of people have them.'

'The way the garage man looked at it when I mentioned Derek. It must have been his. It's gone. Why?'

She was still grinning broadly. It was a wonderful sight. 'Go on! Go on, Mister Detective! "Of all the Morris Minors in all the world you hadda walk into that one!" Or something like that. You can't help yourself, can you? Why should it be Derek's? Because a man looked at it? And why has it gone? Maybe it's been put into the workshops and they are repairing it. Maybe its owner collected it. But don't worry— you're going to go and look, aren't you?'

'Sue—'

'Come on!' She really seemed to be enjoying herself. 'I married you. After all that I knew, I married you. I made up my mind. I can't complain now, no, I won't complain now, because I can see what gets you going and brings you alive. Round you go, Tim. Turn the car. There'll be no living with you unless you follow your whatever-it-is. The cliff fell down and there will be a perfectly logical explanation why that car's been moved. But you need to know. So do it.'

'Sue—'

'Do it, Tim!'

I swung the car round and just missed the opposite pavement. I drove carefully up to the garage, turned in and stopped by the grimy petrol pumps. I got out into the streaming wind, buttoning up my jacket. The signs flapped and rotated. The Morris Minor was no longer there. The second-hand cars were all still there, rooted there, second-hand cars that no one wanted, that God-knew-who wanted, that no one surely could ever want. The dirty kiosk sign, pressed to its grimy windows, obscured the weed-smoking old delinquent within. Closed, it said.

The sign said Closed.

That's odd, I thought, walking towards it, they surely wouldn't close on a Saturday before lunch, not here where every pennyworth of trade must be vital. Besides, I thought I saw a notice, before, saying open from 6.0 a.m. until midnight. I hadn't noticed the Closed sign then but the old codger must have forgotten it. Typical. I mean I only used this place an hour or so ago, not even that, before we got to that awful scene. I expect the old codger will tell me to bugger off for being rude to him. It just shows you, you never know who you'll need just after you've thumbed them in the eye.

The kiosk door opened, though, so they couldn't be closed. Inside, the cans of oil and the peanuts were still stacked on the counter. The place smelt strongly of rolling cigarette tobacco and oily metal mixed with frowst and generations of body odour released from sweaty overalls. I closed the door reluctantly, cutting off the slicing seaside wind.

'Anybody in?'

There were racks of spare parts behind the counter, receding towards the workshop door. Fan-belts and wiper blades mingled with radiator caps and moulded rubber hoses with ribbed cylindrical surfaces like something advertised in a sex-aid magazine. I went up to the counter, banged it and called out again.

'Hello? Shop! Anybody—'

He was down behind the counter, jammed at an odd angle into the constricted wooden space. Blood caked the side of his head, which was pressed against the wooden back wall. The rest of the old codger was piled in a loose heap of arms, body, legs and dirty clothing. The self-rolled cigarette trapped between the first two fingers was still smouldering faintly. If he'd been alive he'd have been conscious that the fag-end was burning his flesh, which it was, but of course he wasn't.

Wasn't conscious, I mean.

Or alive, come to that.

CHAPTER 6

Nobby Roberts was in a terrible state. He paced up and down our living-room without his walking-stick, gesticulating and letting his gingery-red hair stick out on the back of his head. As physiotherapy practice for his leg it was doing him no end of good, but his blood pressure would have driven the Flying Scotsman all the way to Edinburgh. His face was bright red.

'It is,' he said for the umpteenth time that morning, Sunday morning of all mornings, 'the most bloody disgraceful cock-up of all time.'

'Nobby, really,' Sue said calmly, 'you must restrain yourself.'

She was wearing a white rope-twist sweater and jeans and looked like a girl just back from a healthy field game on a spring afternoon. I really don't know how she does it.

He ignored her. He pulled himself up in front of me yet again and twisted his face into a visible snarl. 'You simply cannot be trusted,' he stuttered. 'You are a recidivist. An old lag. You get worse as time goes on. I thought—I thought when you got married that that was it; you'd learnt your lesson. A sigh of relief went round Scotland Yard, I can tell you, when I gave them the news. And yet here you are, not even four months married and you're at it again. Again! You make me look like a bloody fool. A right Charlie. That man Foster was quite jubilant. You—you go down to Hastings on some typical wild-goose chase—typical is the mildest thing I can say about it—taking Sue down with you, literally taking her down with you—I thought she'd restrain you, not egg you on—'

'Nobby,' Sue said, still as sweet as pie, 'why didn't you bring Gillian and the kids with you this morning? We could all have gone to—'

'Bring Gillian? Bring Gillian? Good God, I never let Gillian get involved in my work! When I'm on duty!'

'Ho!' I said. 'Ho, ho! On duty, is it? This is official, then, is it? None of your finger on the nose, friendly chat, nod's as good as a wink to a blind horse—'

'You!' He pointed a finger at me. 'I don't know what to do about you! I really don't! No one does. You go, as I say, to Hastings on a wild goose chase, ignoring what happened the last time you were there—'

'Nobby, that was—'

'Bodies all over the place and policemen assaulted! I'll never forget it!'

'You are exaggerating, Nobby. You are overwrought. Really, as Sue says, you must calm down. Remember your condition.'

'My condition! My condition! Before you can say Jack Robinson there's cottages down the cliff, bodies crushed, there's garage attendants battered to death within minutes of noting your car number down, you have a stand-up row with the same senior police officer, threatening to throw him over a cliff, you ignore police warning notices, you refuse to assist the police in their inquiries—'

'Oh come on, Nobby! Foster and I got on quite well in the end. Not exactly chums but certainly a measure of mutual respect.'

This was true. The atmosphere in Hastings police station, when we finally got there, had been considerably warmer than that at the cliff edge and not only in physical temperature. Sue and I had been given mugs of tea and a friendly WPC put a plate of biscuits on the table in the waiting-room where we were sitting. Foster came in from making phone calls and sat opposite us, his manner conciliatory. Without his raincoat and brushed smooth from his windswept cliff appearance he looked quite respectable.

'Look here,' he said, giving me a straight eye. 'We got off to a bad start last time and I'm sorry it's not got off right this one. I'm obliged to you for agreeing to come here and to make a statement. I've been more than a bit rattled by this business and I'm sure it must have been a shock to you. Both of you. So if it's all right with you I'd like to start off again. No hard feelings. How about it?'

I bowed my head. 'Fair enough. I think an apology is due from me, actually. Bit out of order on the cliff there.'

'Fine.' He didn't dwell on it any more. 'That's forgotten, then. In that case—oh, by the way, I gather that congratulations are in order?'

'Sorry?'

'The marriage? You are now Mr and Mrs Simpson, I believe?'

'Oh.' I smiled. He'd obviously been on the phone to Nobby. 'Yes. Thank you.'

Sue smiled at him. 'Thank you, Inspector.' She was recovering her composure. I hadn't allowed her out of the Jaguar parked in the garage yard, just told her what had happened and waited with her until the police I'd called and, eventually, Foster, arrived. I'd never seen anyone so visibly in a state of consternation. Once he'd absorbed the facts, however, the professional person took over; he sorted out the sequence of events, called up another set of forensic experts to the scene and, popping across to the Jaguar where we were waiting for the occasional word, was very civil. There was a certain look in his eye, not awed exactly but certainly impressed in some way or another, as he'd asked me, politely this time, to come down and make a statement. It was as though he was meeting me for the first time and found it strange. Even now, he watched me carefully as he got the wedding felicitations over and moved on to the next sequence, like a lecturer organizing his slides before the public event.

'Ah,' he said. 'Good. Fine. If I may start at the beginning. Could you just summarize for me how well you knew Sedgwick and what brought you down to Fairlight this morning? So that I can get the full picture?'

I told him, and he listened carefully, making notes. I

showed him the letter and he went off to take a photocopy of it.

'If you don't mind,' he said, coming back and handing me the photocopy, 'I'll keep the original. We can establish where it was written, with any luck.'

'Of course.' I put the photocopy in my pocket.

'Sheep, goats and soap,' Foster repeated carefully. 'You say that's a reference to paintings—Pre-Raphaelites, I think you called them—which would be valuable?'

'Yes. Very valuable.'

'Hm. You—that is, Chief Inspector Roberts was an Art Fraud Squad man, of course. He's made something of a speciality of it, hasn't he?'

'Yes.' I decided it would be tactless to mention my own role in some of Nobby's cases.

'And your bank's investment fund would have been interested in buying these paintings?'

'Yes. Very.'

Foster had scratched his chin thoughtfully. 'You have no indication whether Sedgwick might have approached other parties interested in such paintings?'

'No. I mean I don't know. He might have. In fact he almost certainly would. To make sure he got the best price.'

'Of course. Any ideas on who he might have approached?'

'I'm sorry, I haven't. He could have gone to one of the London specialist galleries like Christopher Wood, one of the big auctioneers, or he might just have tried a private collector or a collector's agent. I haven't seen Derek for three years and then that was at a garden-party. If he picked me out from an old copy of *Art News* he could have been trying everyone. The letter took a bit of time to get to me via my old College. He might have thought that I wasn't going to respond.'

'Hmmm.'

'Tell me—you said he was sniffing things he shouldn't. When we, er, you and I that is, were disagreeing a bit on the cliff edge. I never had Derek down as a drugs type. But that's what you meant?'

Foster had rubbed his chin this time. 'Yes. Well. Let us just say that Sedgwick was under observation and that he had attended certain gatherings where such things were done. Hastings is not exactly the South Bronx or whatever, but such problems have arisen. Mostly within a predictable segment of the population, but not always. And there were, er, certain other aspects.'

'Oh?'

'More tea?' Foster avoided my query carefully. 'I'm afraid the station's been turned over to a vending machine, which is disgraceful. Economies made by public service accountants. Everything pared to the bone.'

'Thanks.'

He made arrangements and plastic cups of tea were brought. He sipped his cautiously as he re-read my fairly brief statement and asked me, again, if I was quite happy to sign it. I was; I had done. He shuffled it a bit, knowing what Sue and I were waiting to hear. He cleared his throat.

'I'm afraid,' he said eventually, 'that it's going to take longer than we thought to retrieve the bodies from the cottage. The work is hampered by the conditions and the weather is worsening.'

'Bodies?'

'Yes. Bodies. There are two for sure. One male, one female. So far.'

'Christ.'

'Very distressing. There is really no point in you being retained here. No point at all. You've given us every assist-ance and we have your full statement. I've been in contact with your—with Chief Inspector Roberts, and have agreed to keep him fully informed. He has expressed a warm personal interest, of course.'

Wonderfully put. No more tactful police spokesman could have existed. A warm personal interest. Warmth was not how I would have described it; explosions are warm but they do not convey warmth. They blow your hat off.

Foster condensed the papers into a file. 'I don't think that we should tax you with identification and so on,' he said. 'Grisly requirement, and in any case, you haven't seen Sedgwick for years. We can manage that otherwise. So—'

He'd made a gesture of finality. Sue and I removed ourselves with relief. Foster even went so far as to escort us to the car. His face peered at mine with that curious expression I'd seen at the cliff edge.

'Go carefully,' he'd said. 'I did assure Chief Inspector Roberts that you were composed enough to drive. I expect he'll be in contact with you, eventually.'

Eventually? Nobby had practically come in with the morning light. It was an awful day, lashing down with rain, cold, miserable, the gardens all dead-looking and rusted with more fallen leaves. I'd rather have stayed in bed. But the certain knowledge that he'd arrive had got us up and organized, so that when he gusted in like a squall on the Fairlight cliff edge we were ready for him. That hadn't pleased him either.

He stuck his face towards me again. 'You and Foster? Mutual respect? The man is staggered. Numbed by you. Didn't you realize? He said he felt he was in the company of a necrogenic phenomenon.'

'There's no need to be offensive, Nobby.'

'Everywhere you go, bodies abound. Especially in the Hastings area. What is the man to think? And your remarks. I mean, it's extraordinary.'

'What's extraordinary? I don't like the tone of this, Nobby. I didn't make insulting remarks about poor old Derek. If anyone did it was Foster. Poor taste when you think that he can't rise from the dead to defend himself, isn't it?'

Nobby stopped. He blinked at me. 'Oh my God.' The gingery-pink of his freckled face faded suddenly.

'What's up?'

'Derek Sedgwick isn't dead. Not, at least, so far as we know.'

'What?'

'I'm awfully sorry, Tim. I completely overran myself in my state of—state of whatever. I meant to tell you when I arrived. The body of the man wasn't Derek Sedgwick. Not at all. It was a large man, fattish, not Sedgwick. An Asiatic type. Not European.'

'Not Derek? You're sure?' I suddenly had a vision of Foster, tamping down the statement papers with an air of finality. Of course; he must have known.

Nobby licked his lips and glanced quickly at Sue. Then he shook his head. 'Actually, it's unmistakable, apparently. The body is a Japanese.'

'Japanese? The woman too?' I felt a series of emotions but mainly enormous relief; Derek must have been away somewhere. What luck the man had; with a great bound of inner hope I realized that the Pre-Raphaelite paintings might still be available. All was not lost; the chase was still on.

Nobby shook his head. 'The woman was not Japanese. In fact, she has been identified as a friend of Sedgwick's called Monica Haines. There is no sign of Sedgwick anywhere. Due to—to all these events, and his missing car, we are looking for him to help us in our inquiries.'

'Good heavens. We?'

He pursed his lips. 'Due to the possible association with art or art theft, and, I need hardly add, your involvement, I have been assigned in an advisory capacity to this case. Which is why I am wasting my Sunday break in this manner.'

'Oh dear. Well, I'm sorry, Nobby. I say, I do believe the girl he brought to that garden-party was called Monica. What on earth were she and a Japanese doing in that cottage, without Derek?'

Nobby glanced at Sue and blushed slightly. 'I'm afraid that seems fairly obvious.'

'Good grief. You don't mean—'

'I do.'

'God save us! You mean when—when the cliff gave way they were—' I couldn't help it—'making the earth move?'

'Tim! Really!'

Nobby actually scowled. 'The cliff did not give way. That cliff had been thoroughly checked and even shored up by the local authorities. That's why Foster found you so extraordinary. I mean, it's astounding. You make these remarks and then you blandly go off and find a murdered man at the garage. Probably within minutes of the event. No wonder Foster decided to treat you with kid gloves. I just can't credit it.'

'Remarks? What remarks?' I stared at him, bewildered. 'What do you mean, "I say these things"?'

'Don't deny it. What you said to Foster was too much. It really was. Over the top.'

'Nobby.' Sue was sweetly mystified but clearly becoming impatient. 'What remarks of Tim's are you talking about? We really haven't the faintest idea what you're saying.'

'About the dynamite. What else? How on earth did Tim guess that while that Jap and the bird were somewhat occupied in the cottage someone blew the bloody cliff clean away from under them?'

CHAPTER 7

Quite a lot of art galleries open on Sunday afternoon. Not those in Cork Street of course, or anywhere where they're aiming to sell really expensive Fine Art rather than impulse-purchase or tourist hackery, and not very many on a foul dark Sunday afternoon in November. The street in Hammersmith where the Vergam Gallery was located was almost half way back to West Kensington, not far from the North End Road where Burne-Jones once lived in his Grange with a loyal but alienated wife. It was there that the Burne-Joneses entertained the tormented William and Jane Morris to tea on Sundays while the children roamed in the garden. I don't really share Jeremy's (and Bidlake's) jaundiced view of Ned Jones, as his friends called him. The problem for the poor man was one of sex, as it is for so many of us, and as it was for Morris, Rossetti and even Holman Hunt. The only one of that mob to get himself well organized was Millais, and that was only after the stupendous upheaval and scandal of extricating Effie from her unconsummated marriage to Ruskin.

I squinted up and down the street in ruminative mood. They knocked down the Grange in the late 'fifties and built blocks of contemporary apartments of GLC design all over the lawns, but the style of the area still remains predominantly grey-bricked Victorian, in rows of what were once desirable suburban terraces. The Vergam Gallery was off the Hammersmith Road in a street of mixed houses and shops, all steadily being improved by paint and structural rehabilitation of a consciously period type. It was closed.

'Damn,' I said, rattling the door-handle a bit. 'I should think that this Jane Lardner must have a flat above the gallery by the look of it.'

The gallery was adapted from a double-fronted shop with large windows. Plain cream walls were covered in some sort of fabric and there were the usual spotlights in clusters attached to lighting bars on the ceiling. Modern paintings, prints and batiks hung on the walls. To me that area of London is a barren wasteland, lost between the built-over playing fields of St Paul's School and the railway lines which slice West Kensington off from Earls Court like so many cheesewires through a block of cheddar. Technically it's Brook Green but really I'm not sure where it is.

'The police,' said Sue realistically and for the second time, 'will have been here already. I don't think, even if she were here, that we'd be welcome.'

She then let her teeth chatter for a bit to make me feel guilty. Although we were both well wrapped up and the car was not far away, it was penetratingly cold. A filthy wind full of dirt and sweet papers swirled up off the pavement in bleak gusts. We should have been sitting by the fire in Onslow Gardens, reading the Sunday papers and dozing, but she was doing this to make me happy. Well, actually, she was doing this because she wanted to and because it would make me happy as well. We'd worked that one out pretty soon after Nobby had left, uttering threats and warnings about full cooperation or else, but making confident noises about how he'd find Derek Sedgwick before we could do any real damage.

'The police,' I replied, also for the second time, 'will have been unlikely to get positive help from any associate of Derek's. Derek's life was far too close to too many dodgy enterprises for that. From what Foster said, this Jane Lardner might be one of them. The gallery looks pretty desperate to me. I mean, how do you pay VAT, the rent and uniform business rate on these premises out of a motley collection of duds like those in there?'

I indicated the artwork inside as I leant on the bell and rattled the door-handle again. There was an abstract in the window that was compounded of every cliché you could

think of; there was a minimalist print in mainly white paper
with a single curved line in green, entitled *Landscape VI* and
there was a batik of a piece of bread. But I won't go on;
you've doubtless seen acres of similar confections; there's
an awful lot of art about. The good thing about our presence
was that we'd made it with absolute agreement, indeed with
Sue positively egging me on. It seemed difficult to believe
that marriage could make such a change. In the past,
confronted with collapsed cottages fatally embracing a mis-
cegenating Japanese and a garage booth sheltering the fresh
corpse of a recently argumentative old codger, both virtually
discovered by me, she'd have gone off not into hysterics but
into coldly discouraging disapprobation. The exceptions to
that behaviour were when she'd had a personal interest in
the artwork I was chasing after, and in this case I had a
strong suspicion that the Pre-Raphaelite Brotherhood were
largely responsible for her lack of obstruction. No, on reflection, that was unfair. I thought about her remarks at breakfast during the week and again in the car going down to
Hastings. Sue had always had a strong sense of partnership;
now that it was official, it seemed to be even stronger. I
looked at her with affection.

'Wherever Derek's got to,' I said, 'and whyever he's made
himself scarce, we must make sure we don't miss out on his
sheep, goats and soap.'

She grinned at me. Just then a door opened at the back
of the gallery and a woman stared out at us from behind an
office desk. She was reasonably tall, about five feet eight I'd
say, and dark, but skinny. She wore a cheap donkey-brown
suit which had a skirt hiked above the knees, emphasizing
her bony legs. I stared back at her hopefully, trying to adopt
a friendly, encouraging expression. Sue put a hand to her
face to protect her eyes from another gust of wet, grimy
wind. The woman waited, seeming to hesitate, and then
indicated the door, miming the word Closed. I shook my
head vigorously and pointed at her, then at myself. Reluctantly she came forward and there was a pause while she

unlocked and opened the door a few inches, putting her head to the gap.

'I'm sorry, we're closed.' The voice was flat, with that slight London, half-cockney intonation that so many of the fashion-conscious seem to adopt these days.

'Jane Lardner?'

'Yes.' She looked at me suspiciously, then at Sue.

'I'm very sorry to bother you but we're looking for Derek. Derek Sedgwick.'

Her expression altered. Her head went back a bit and she looked down her nose. 'He's not here. Who are you?'

'I'm a friend of Derek's. He wrote to me to come and see him. My name is Tim Simpson.'

'Oh.' She opened the door a little wider. 'I'm sorry, but Derek isn't here.'

'Do you know where I could find him?'

'I'm sorry.' She had a neutral expression, now. 'He went to Spain and didn't say when he'd be back.'

'Spain?'

'Yes. He has a place he's doing up in the north. Navarra. You're not police, then?'

'Police? Good heavens no. Should we be?'

'Oh, er, no. They've been here twice to look for him. Apparently the cottage has gone over the cliffs at Fairlight.'

'Cottage?'

'Yeah. Derek had a sort of squat in a farm cottage near the cliffs.' She grinned slightly. 'It's fallen over.'

'Oh dear. Well, actually, we knew. We went down there yesterday to find him and we saw it. This is Sue, my wife.'

The two women smiled faintly at each other. It came to me, looking at Jane Lardner, that she either was or had been involved with Derek Sedgwick and not just professionally as his gallery owner. Don't ask me why or how I knew, but I knew. She was the antithesis of Derek apart from her skinny physique, cool to his hot, clean to his grubby, but she'd been his. I knew it. Was this why I was dissembling, waiting to hear what she said? She was one of Derek's women, I was suddenly sure of that, his paintings would be inside, perhaps this would be his London pad. Although, clearly, he mostly lived at Fairlight, otherwise he could have contacted me here in London. What was the set-up? A part-time arrangement?

'You better come in for a moment.' The accent was better, the sub-cockney was fading. 'It's freezing out there.'

Thanking her, we trooped in, Sue first. The shelter made the gallery feel warm for a moment and I enjoyed it before the temperature of the unheated area reasserted itself. Some of the paintings were very bright, with splashes of yellow and red that cheered the November light.

'It's very kind of you. I suppose there's no way of contacting him?'

She shook her head. Sue looked at her expectantly for a moment before speaking. 'Jane—I hope you don't mind my calling you Jane—we're very worried because Tim had a letter from Derek suggesting a meeting and now this awful thing has happened.'

Jane Lardner blinked. 'You mean about the couple in the cottage?'

'Yes. Isn't it dreadful? Did you know either of them?'

'Me? Good heavens, no.' The tone was offended, resentful. 'I never got involved with Derek's Fairlight lets. He quite often let people use the place while he was away just to help sub the rent. Not that the rent was anything much; awful dump. How anyone could live that close to the edge always beat me, but Derek said it was OK. It was damp, though; bloody damp.'

The tone was false. She was lying. I was willing to bet she must have known of Monica Haines even if she'd never met her, even if Derek had kept them apart. Involuntarily I glanced up at the ceiling; maybe he was up there somewhere, staying out of sight.

'Did Derek still have his Morris Minor?'

The question made her blink before she nodded. 'The police asked that too. I said I thought he did. I mean, he hardly ever used it. When he came to London he caught the train. But he used it around Hastings, I guess. It was pretty decrepit. I can't think why anyone would want to pinch it.'

'No.' There was an awkward pause. Why had she let us in instead of giving us a negative and sending us on our way? What did she want to know? She was behaving in much too detached a mode; surely someone normal would have chatted madly about the events, the garage man, the speculations. Her face was thin but smooth, the skin drawn tight over high cheekbones and jawline. She had the sort of figure and height that women would find elegant; how on earth did Derek do it?

'It's been frightfully embarrassing.' Her tone modulated again, more classy, more woman-of-the-world. 'I mean, the police and everything; I've handled Derek's stuff for a long time but it's been no more than that—have you seen his latest stuff?'

'Er, no, I haven't.'

She gestured towards one wall of the gallery, where the brightest, reddest and yellowest pictures hung. She turned and went closer to them. I followed curiously.

'They're gouaches,' Sue stated, cocking her head to one side.

'Yeah. He went to New Orleans. It went really well. I mean, he sold quite a few there and brought some back. I've sold a few; these are what's left.'

'They're very confident.' Sue's voice was professional, assessing. I looked closer. The colours were too pure for me, with my typical muddy British attitude to art, but there was no doubting the boldness of the drawing. One painting depicted a huge open yellow car with vast tail wings, a real Yankee job, in which a large man with a cigar had his arm round two leggy girls. The car was progressing down an equally colourful street with big red signs and a tangle of windows. It was titled *Bourbon Street Parade*.

'How long ago was he there?' I could visualize Derek,

tall, grubby and shorted, mingling with a New Orleans crowd, his knobby knees crinkling.

'Last winter. He finished some of the work off in Spain.' She turned towards the rear door of the gallery and, almost as if on cue, a man in blue jeans and a red wool sweatshirt stepped through, closing the door behind him, pushing his hand through thick, light, corn-coloured hair. His skin was sunburnt and his movements muscular.

'Hi,' he said unemotionally, looking more at Jane Lardner than at us, though I caught a quick, assessing glance in my direction.

An American, obviously.

'This is Doug.' Jane Lardner's manner brightened. 'Doug, this is Tim and Sue Simpson. They're friends of Derek's, looking for him. They were down at Fairlight and saw the cottage. You know? The thing the police were here about?'

'Oh, sure.' The man called Doug came across and shook hands. 'Hi. Bad news, eh?'

'Doug's been handling Derek's affairs in the States,' Jane Lardner explained. 'He's done a terrific job over there.' She gestured at the colours on the wall. 'In New Orleans. It seems to have done Derek's painting a power of good.'

'He's great.' The man called Doug held eye-contact with me, blue and rather penetrating, far more than was for some reason comfortable. 'It really did go well. Derek seems to get a kick out of painting over with us. He goes for it.'

The voice was soft, pleasant, low-toned but detached, as so many Americans seem to us. Jane Lardner was looking at him closely, as though following what he said word by word. He flashed her a quick smile of complicity before looking at Sue with interest.

I wondered how long he had been behind the door.

'Are you over for long?' I threw out the safest question I could think of, watching him, wondering how close he and Jane Lardner were.

'Just a few days.' He took his eyes off Sue to look at me.

'I came for another look at these—' he gestured at the wall—'a few days ago. I have kind of a personal interest in them. If they don't sell here I'll take them back to the States. I come over regularly. I handle a few of your British artists over there.'

'I see. Very good.'

'Doug's done a terrific job for Derek.' Jane Lardner had adopted a bright, front-woman manner. 'Really he has. It's made a tremendous impact.'

On what? I nearly asked. There was an awkward pause. For a moment the four of us stood uncertainly, staring at each other. I wondered where this Doug, the man from New Orleans, was staying, but decided it would be impertinent to ask.

'Well,' I said, to break the silence, 'I'm sorry we've missed him. Is there no way of contacting him in Spain?'

'Only by post, to the local post office.' Jane Lardner's reply came quickly. 'The place is a disused stable he's been converting, up in those rocky hills. Awful. He likes it because he can live there for nothing and get pissed for a quid on the local plonk, but it's bitter up there in the winter. It gives him undisturbed working time though, or it's supposed to.'

I was about to ask if anyone ever went with him but thought better of it as an image of Monica Haines came to mind. 'Well. Thanks. If he does phone in or something would you let him know that I've been trying to find him?'

She gave me a mocking stare. 'He's never phoned in, to my knowledge. Never. If he does, and he won't, I'll have a lot more to tell him than that. A lot more.'

'You sure will.' Doug's voice was still neutral, un-emotional. 'I hope he won't be too upset by all this. He was fond of that cottage, did a lot of work there. He often told us about it. I would love to have seen it.' He grinned. 'No chance of that now, eh?'

'Er, no.' I thought about dynamite and decided to think no more. What Nobby tells me is always in strict confidence. 'Well, thanks anyway.' There didn't seem to be anything more to say. Doug had moved slightly so that he and Jane Lardner faced us expectantly. It was obviously time to leave. Sue and I moved back to the door. 'Thanks,' I said again. 'Sorry to have disturbed you.'

'No problem.' Doug's manner was still neutral.

'Oh no.' Jane Lardner came out of what seemed to be a trance. 'Sorry I can't help. Especially in this awful weather.'

I clanged the door shut after Sue had stepped through. The freezing wind raced up the grey street, whipping us quickly back to the car where we belted ourselves back into the protected interior with relief.

'That was a strange do,' I said to Sue, sitting without starting the engine. 'I don't think we got one half, no, not one quarter, of the story we could have been told.'

She ignored me. She was staring straight ahead, through the windscreen.

'If,' she said eventually, 'if he was in Spain, or even knew he was going there, why did he ask you down to Fairlight?'

I opened my mouth, but she went right on without even noticing. 'And if,' she continued, 'if he saw you in an article in *Art News*, why didn't he write to you care of the Bank, or the Fund, here in London, instead of via your old College, which he knew would take time and wouldn't fix a firm date? I seem to remember that article showed the Fund's acquisitions, chapter and verse, all about them. Why did he write to you via Cambridge, of all places?'

She turned to look at me with puzzled eyes but I was beaming at her. I started the engine.

'Do you know,' I said, 'you're starting to think like me, at last.'

Her face puckered. 'All right, wise guy,' she said. 'Just because you made me look like an idiot back at that garage there's no need to get fresh. I've always known how you think. I have to start from the bottom, don't I?'

CHAPTER 8

Jeremy White did one of his two-steps up and down the office. For a Monday morning he was moving quickly, but then, with a face as congested as his and a body as tense, rapid movement constituted the best form of relief.

'My dear Tim! This is appalling! It's happened again! Again!'

'I know. It has indeed, Jeremy. Not my fault, of course. The meeting of the Art Fund sparked all this off.'

He stopped in mid-hop.

'What? What? You—you exonerate yourself? You try to avoid the clear, the absolutely crystal clear role as— as catalyst—that you have played?' His face as he stopped in front of me was a mask of aggressive inquiry, rather like a barrister hamming it up to the equivalent of the Centre Court at the Old Bailey.

'My dear Jeremy. You must be well aware that without your interference neither I nor Geoffrey would have set in train a pursuit of a Pre-Raphaelite or any other kind of painting. We would simply have let things be. But you insisted, you wouldn't be deterred, you absolutely insisted that our cash—'

'Me! Me! You blame me! My God! That's rich! Rich! I hate the bloody Pre-Raphaelites. I knew no good would come out of it. Digging up graves and boiling down horses. Freezing girls in stone cold baths. Unhealthy. The whole bunch of them. Swilling down drugs with pints of whisky. As for wives and paramours—'

'Jeremy! We agreed to leave Rossetti out of it. Hunt boiled down a horse to determine the bone structure of the skeleton. And Ophelia—'

'Disgusting! The neighbours complained of the stench. I would have, too.'

'Jeremy—'

'Stop! Stop!' He held up a dramatic hand. 'Enough. The merits of the art investment are immaterial. The fact, the indisputable fact, is that your methods and contacts, if they can be called that, have once again led you into the criminal world. As so often has happened before. Here we are, a bank, a respectable merchant bank of long standing—'

'Operating in the world of insider dealing, insurance swindles, currency frauds, takeover scams, bribery, third-party commissions, arms dealers, commodity confidence trickery, property hypes—'

'Tim! Really! Really! You shock me. Really you do.'

'Art is a currency somewhat like money these days, Jeremy. Everyone who handles the stuff, or wants to, must be treated with caution. There are vast numbers of honest people among whom the criminal few circulate with ease. With money the ground rules are more clearly laid down, that's all. At least they should be, but I'm not at all sure that they are. Look at the Guinness affair, look at—'

'No I will not! I have had quite enough of these recent City scandals. I was hoping we could get on with our business without looking at those.'

I grinned at him. His tone had taken on a rueful tinge. At least he'd stopped two-stepping. He scowled at me. 'Have some coffee?'

'God. I thought you'd never ask.'

It was a peace-offering. I sat down and he clambered behind his desk to sit facing me. His secretary brought coffee and gave me a faint wink before leaving. He poured out and peered at me gloomily. 'I suppose you'll never consider abandoning this—this line of inquiry?'

I sipped from the china cup, feeling soothed. 'You know how it is, Jeremy. It usually won't abandon me.'

'What about Sue? What does she say?'

'Amazing. She's very positive about the whole thing. Before we were married she'd have thrown a blue fit. But this time she's right alongside. Perhaps because she's been in on events from the start. Seen how blameless I am.'

'Blameless? My God! Things are getting worse. If Sue is going to start aiding and abetting you in these matters they'll need a new department at Scotland Yard. What about Nobby Roberts? What does he say?'

'More sorrow than anger, Jeremy, more sorrow than anger. Nobby, after a certain vigour of expression, simmered down. I rather think Sue's participation helped there. It gave, shall we say, a certain respectability to what might otherwise have been interpreted as a raffish escapade.'

He gave me an old-fashioned look. 'You had this letter by the time you came to our meeting?'

'That very morning, it came. That very morning.'

He pursed his lips. 'I thought you were laying it on a bit thick. Thought you'd got something up your sleeve. Enjoying yourself, weren't you?'

'Merely reacting to a fairly intense pressure from you, Jeremy.'

'Pah! We have to keep up the pace with the fund, Tim. We can't sit back. I would never have thought that Geoffrey would go overboard so completely, though. The Pre-Raphaelites! My God!'

'Bourgeois romance, Jeremy. The Pre-Raphaelites' appeal is to the middle-class romantic virtues, according to Gay Daly. She wrote *The Pre-Raphaelites in Love*.'

'Dear Heaven.'

'What she says has a lot to it, Jeremy. It explains Geoffrey's emotions. The Pre-Raphaelite paintings have a lot of uncomfortable imagery for our rational, sexually liberated days. I'm sure Mrs Thatcher would like the Pre-Raphaelites. Victorian virtues and moral lessons; the nation still yearns for them under all that flummery and computer-aided dating. Quite apart from the painting technique, of course, which is painfully hardworking and technically admirable. Modern art training discounts it entirely.'

'I hate it.'

'Enough of the art lecture, though. Can I have some more coffee?'

He refilled my cup, looking at me steadily over the pot. When he'd finished he stirred his own fresh cup and frowned thoughtfully. 'Why do you think this Sedgwick wrote to you via your old College?'

'I've thought about that. Either it was to appeal to an old relationship, which doesn't really make sense because there wasn't one, or else it was to buy time. That doesn't make sense, either. I mean, he could simply have waited for a couple of days before posting the letter.'

'But for Heaven's sake, Tim, anyone normal wanting to contact you these days would simply have phoned you here at the Bank, or left a message with your secretary.'

'There was no phone at the cottage.'

'Good grief! You mean it's inconceivable that a public phone-booth could be found nearby, do you? Eh? Or a friend's phone, or a phone at a nearby farmhouse?'

'Well—maybe. But a letter is cheap.'

'No.' His voice had suddenly gone sharp.

'What?'

'A letter is evidence. A letter can be shown in evidence. Or a copy of it. It can be used.'

Jeremy is no innocent, never has been. I nodded at him, slowly. 'You mean it could be used as evidence of action, to stimulate someone dragging his feet? To play him off against me? Or as evidence of an entrée to the world of art investment, to give credibility, to convince someone?'

'Precisely, Tim.'

'Dear me. The plot thickens. I know that Derek Sedgwick wouldn't hesitate to do that sort of thing, old College or no old College. But there's so much to explain. I wonder where the hell he is?'

'Not in Spain. I'd bet on that.' Jeremy took a deep draught of his coffee. 'That Lardner woman is lying; I'm sure you're right about that.'

'Which raises another whole set of questions. Anyway,

the police have the best chance of finding him, I suppose. Nothing much we can do there.'

'No.' He gave me a sharp look. 'Weren't thinking of it, were you?'

'No, no. Just curious, you know. It would help to explain a lot.'

'Tim!'

I waved a placatory palm at him. 'Keep cool, Jeremy. Nobby Roberts is sure they'll find him. And Sue is convinced that the Lardner woman is no source of information in that direction.'

'Sue? She's not off on some trail on your behalf, is she?'

'Oh no. Sue's very busy with a forthcoming exhibition. She's gone off to Reading today to check arrangements for the loan of two Stanley Spencers or something.'

'Ah.' He relaxed slightly. 'Well, I have to attend to a trustees' meeting at ten. I do hope I can rely on you to stay out of trouble for the moment?'

'Absolutely, Jeremy. You know me.'

'That is precisely the reason I asked the question.'

I pulled a face at him. There's no other way to deal with Jeremy when he's in one of those moods.

CHAPTER 9

The church of St Clement stands above the congested narrow High Street of Hastings Old Town. The original mediæval part is choked into the narrow Bourne Valley, where a jumble of cottages, houses and shops are crammed together round the long sunless street. Off the surprisingly straight thoroughfare go the alleys they call twittens and courtyards with steep rising steps that lift you to further back terraces and closed courts, but the church of St Clements stands in a clearing partly created by a German bomb in 1940. The church itself is very old, of grey chequered stone with Gothic window tracery, a large church to fit the more prosperous west side of the Old Town. It is one into which a substantial congregation could fit, but when Rossetti married Elizabeth Siddal there in 1860 there was no one present, not even a friend or relation. Strangers had to sign the register as witnesses. Apart from this and the fact that Elizabeth Siddal was chronically sick and Rossetti subconsciously desired release from her by her death, it must have been a cheerful occasion.

Gusts of icy rain drenched the small shopfronts and filled the gutters. I had left the car back behind the High Street in a park bounded by fish and chip shops, closed amusement arcades and ice-cream kiosks that, when open, sold sticks of rock. The drive down had been uneventful but I felt keyed up like a schoolboy playing truant, a feeling brought on by my quick sneak out of the Bank after Jeremy had gone to his trustees' meeting. Visions of Derek Sedgwick kept coming to me, memories of his past career and its occasional entanglement with mine. It's a small world, as the old bores say, and you never can tell the way things will go. Always be nice to those you meet on the way up; you'll meet the same mob on your way down.

As soon as you get away from the sea front, the character of the town changes. I dodged along the High Street past wine bars and a proper bakery next to a fishmonger's. Antique shops began to make their appearance, dusty books filled a window, prints, paintings and pottery became evident. Several shops were for sale. A metal dustbin stood outside an ironmonger's and next to this was a double-fronted shop like Jane Lardner's gallery, but smaller, darker because of the narrowness of the street. I fell in through the doorway with a splash of rain, clanging an old-fashioned bell that jangled for a second or two as I looked at the art on the walls around me.

If Jane Lardner's gallery was of marginal commercial viability, this one was inscrutable. Nearly all the artists whose work hung on the walls must have been local. I did recognize work by two RAs and one Cork Street performer, but mainly they were of regional interest. A wood and metal horse of cubist design occupied the central space. There were a lot of limited-edition prints, the sort of local landscape stuff that sells for thirty quid a sheet. Yet the desk at the end and the office equipment beside it looked fairly new, clean and efficient.

Behind the office desk a tall, bright blonde girl was rising uncertainly to her feet. Her thick brilliant-yellow hair was tied up above her head in a huge red bandanna like a hat that a Hollywood Brazilian might have worn. It must have taken her up to over six feet tall. A loose dark robe printed with yellow bananas hung round her. She was incredibly exotic, with a pale clear skin, high cheekbones and large brown eyes that, opened wide, stared at me in amazement.

'Hello, Amanda,' I said cheerfully.

She gaped at me. 'Tim? Tim Simpson?'

'Amanda? Amanda Stanley? Have I the pleasure?'

'I don't believe it! Ee by gum! Tim Simpson! You old—you—you old devil!'

I advanced decorously upon her and planted a kiss on

her cheek, which was dead level with my mouth. She's a big girl, is Amanda Stanley.

She gave me a brief hug. 'Well, well! It's not often a poor Stretford girl like me gets the honour of a visit from the great man himself, tha knows.' The northern accent was over-emphasized but genuine; Amanda Stanley was a Manchester girl. I grinned at her with pleasure; she was a great sight. The hair dye business must have loved her.

'What are you doing here? I suppose you'd like a cup of coffee?'

'Love one.'

She gave me an amused look and turned to an electric kettle by her photocopier and typewriter. 'Using a girl as you always did, Tim.' Her smile belied the reproach.

'Oh, surely. Not me?'

'Yes, yes. My God, it's been a long time. Let me see, the last time we were absolutely alone together was—was—'

Was back of the changing-rooms at Sale Rugby Ground, I thought, about, Christ, about eight years ago, was it that long? But it wouldn't be gentlemanly or tactful to refer to that occasion.

'Was back of the changing-rooms at Sale Rugby Ground,' she said, accusingly, 'a hell of a long time ago. After the match, when you were all so full of ale, remember? You stripped me off like a peeled banana.' She gesticulated at the yellow crescents on her gown.

'Oh, really, Amanda—'

'Don't "oh really Amanda" me!' She poured boiling water on to Nescafé in two mugs. 'I've never forgotten it! Never had the chance to give you a talking-to about that! Never been alone together since. My God, you were in a hurry!'

I took a steaming mug from her. 'You weren't exactly unenthusiastic yourself,' I murmured.

'Well, I knew I was for it, didn't I? There'd have been no stopping you, short of a bulldozer!'

I blushed and she grinned at me affectionately. 'I'm not saying it's a bad memory, Tim.'

I looked into the steaming liquid she'd handed me. 'You went off after that. Your mother, wasn't it? I tried to contact you, but then—'

I left the sentence in mid-air. Amanda Stanley had been a rugger-bird in my early days, one of the Sale Rugby Club's gang of local girls, the star of them for a while. I was playing for Blackheath on that occasion, I think, and there'd been a hell of a thrash after the match up at Sale. The events in the back of the changing-rooms had been caused by excitement, alcohol, and a powerful mutual attraction. The day afterwards her mother fell ill and Amanda had disappeared, back to neighbouring Stretford to tend to her. By the time she resurfaced events had moved on, as they quite simply do. I was away somewhere pursuing my work as a consultant—it was before I joined Jeremy at the Bank—and she moved south to end up in Maida Vale.

'Then you got married,' she said. 'To that junk market girl, Carol.'

'Yes. And divorced. As you know.'

'Sure. But now you've married again.' She smiled at me. 'I wish you luck, Tim.'

'Thanks. But with you—'

'With me,' she said, putting down her mug and walking across to the windows that looked out on to the street, 'with me it was Derek. Derek Sedgwick.' She sighed, her face away from me, and put her hands on the back of her hips, elbows out, to stretch, leaning backwards, like the weary Mariana in Johnny Millais's painting, seductive but tired, staring not through a brilliantly coloured stained-glass window derived from Merton College Chapel but at the slanting gusts of rain falling on to the roofs of cars along the pavement. 'That was why you came here, wasn't it? Not to see me. To ask me about Derek?'

I nodded dumbly. I never could work out how Derek Sedgwick collected his girls. Art was part of it. Amanda was a good artist in her own right, not brilliant, not great, but as good as most of those on her own gallery walls. She lived with Derek for two years in the Maida Vale days, teaching at a local college while he tried to wheel and deal down Kilburn High Street and into the Edgware Road. She met him at a rugger match somewhere, or after one. How the hell she'd tolerated him for so long mystified me because she was bright and a real looker. Somehow the dyed blonde hair suited her, even though it was so obviously straight from the bottle. But Derek must have had something, some promise or charm or excitement that got her and all the others going, otherwise how could it have happened? Thin men can do these things.

'I thought perhaps—' my throat seemed choked and I had to clear it—'perhaps you might, you know, have seen him recently.' This was embarrassing; as far as I knew, the proximity of Amanda in the Old Town to Derek at Fairlight five or six miles away was coincidental. After they'd broken up she got a job teaching art at Hastings Technical College and had been down here ever since, starting up the shop-gallery when education cuts reduced her teaching to part-time. I heard this via an RA whose work she sometimes sold and who seemed to take more than a passing interest in her. Derek had only come down to Fairlight comparatively recently; two years at the most.

She gave me a crooked smile. 'Seen him recently? Derek? He's always in and out. Trying to get me to sell things. Not always his things. No bloody sensitivity at all. He knew I didn't like him; we didn't end up friends.' She gave me another understanding smile, as one who has had a relation-ship break up to another with the same experience. 'I didn't want to see him again but he often came in, dirty and thin. Usually with a scrubber from London. It was humiliating.'

'Why didn't you chuck him out? Ban him?'

A rueful look and a gesture at the walls came from her. 'He brought things I could sell. On commission. I live over the shop, you know. It's bloody awful keeping this place going. I don't know where Derek got them but there were things I couldn't refuse. A drawing by John Nash. A Gilbert Spencer. Things like that.'

'Those would sell here? He didn't take them to London?'

She gave me a look. 'It's not all unemployed fishermen in Hastings, Tim. I do have some good local customers, for good things. I had to swallow my pride and take them. The bastard wanted me to go to bed with him when he brought a Stanley Spencer in, but I soon made myself plain about that.' She wrinkled her nose in distaste. 'Dirty brute. I'd have given him such a belting his ardour would've been permanently switched off. He left the Spencer and I sold it, though; five thousand quid.'

'Wasn't that cheap?'

'It was a drawing. And no questions asked.' She took her hands off her hips and walked back slowly to her coffee. 'It's always been my luck, Tim. Just my luck.' She cocked her head sideways to look at me reflectively. 'Here you are, now, famous and prosperous and remarried. I got Derek Sedgwick, then this rattletrap of a place.'

'I'm not famous. And you're a great girl, Amanda. So you've heard all about the Fairlight cottage?'

She grunted. 'Who hasn't? The whole of Hastings is talking about it. Biggest story since the hurricane. Don't ask me who the Jap was, I've no idea. But I think the girl was Monica Haines. One of Derek's scrubbers.'

'And the garage thing? Did Derek still drive that old Morris Minor?'

'Oh yes. Always.' She looked out at the wet street. 'He'd park it right there.'

'His gallery in London—Jane Lardner—says he's in Spain.'

She gave a great snort of derision. 'Spain! Jane Lardner! She would, the stuck-up bitch! She'd say anything to protect Derek. There's no sour grapes, Tim, I never handled Derek's own paintings, I couldn't stand them, but she's a prize specimen. Derek really fancied that conquest. A lawyer's daughter, don't you know, ever so superior and with money to back her up. She doesn't even have to make a living from that place. You could see he was really chuffed, having it off with a piece like that, even though she's as skinny as a whippet, but then of course he buggered it up by keeping that Monica Haines on his list and Jane Lardner found out. Chucked him out of the flat over the Brook Green place. That's one of the reasons he finished up down here at Fairlight. Worse luck.' Her face was sour. 'Derek Sedgwick fouls up everything he handles, Tim. It was my bad luck to have met him in the first place.'

I put my coffee mug back on her desk. 'Amanda—has a policeman called Foster been to see you?'

'Jerry Foster? No. Why? Should he? He normally only comes in after stolen goods.'

I took the photocopy of Derek's letter out of my wallet and handed it to her. 'I got that from Derek last week. Does it mean anything to you?'

She sipped her coffee and read it, wrinkling her eyebrows in concentration until she got near the end and they raised themselves as her eyes went round. 'Sheep, goats and soap! The artful bastard! He's saying he's got some Pre-Raphaelite paintings, is he?'

'He seems to be.'

'Rubbish! Derek Sedgwick? Pre-Raphaelites? I can tell you, Tim, and I know I don't have to, that Pre-Raphaelites are bloody scarce! I can't see Derek getting his cheap bony hands on one of those!'

'No?'

'No! Who'd trust Derek with a thing like that?'

I had to shake my head. I was hoping she might have been able to tell me. There was no real reason, of course; I guessed that Derek wasn't one of her favourite people and Derek wasn't likely to confide in her. Come to think of it, Derek didn't confide much in any of his lady friends; there was too much to hide for him to do that. But I'd hoped that Amanda Stanley, being local and close and involved in the rather incestuous art world, might have known something, some clue I could trail after. I still looked at her hopefully, catching an expression of mingled indignation and amusement at me, blown in by the rain and the doings of Derek Sedgwick.

'I don't know,' I said, in answer to her question. 'I hadn't even kept up with him. But you never could tell what hares Derek was chasing. He seems to have been painting in New Orleans, though how the hell he got there must he another interesting story.'

'Not nearly as interesting as having his cottage blown off the cliff with two people in it and his garage man murdered while his decrepit old car was stolen.'

'True. It would take a lot to beat that story.'

She was still looking at me. 'Rumour has it, Tim, that you were the last man to buy petrol off old Bill Bengate before he was done in.'

'Oh, has it? The police station at Hastings must leak like a sieve.'

She grinned. 'It does. Jerry Foster gets hopping mad about it, but you know what local gossip is like. Is it true, by the way?'

'About the garage man? I don't know. It could be. I wasn't gone much more than three-quarters of an hour or so before I dropped in on the way back from the cliffs.' She obviously knew the local CID enough to call Foster by his Christian name. That wasn't surprising; the force are always checking antique shops and galleries for stolen art works and I could imagine the local rozzers wouldn't need much of an excuse to drop in and chat up Amanda Stanley. In hopes. 'Trade would have had to be really bad for no one to call in for fuel in all that time.'

She shrugged. 'Old Bill Bengate's garage wasn't very successful, Tim. From what I've been told, anyway.'

I finished my coffee with regret. 'Well. Sorry to have bothered you, Amanda. It was a good excuse to come and see you, though, wasn't it?'

She grinned at that. I suppose she had a lot of men who

invented excuses to come and see her. Although they would not have stirred up memories, both pleasant and unpleasant, and current realities like me. Was that it? Was that why I'd sneaked off from the Bank like a truant schoolboy? Out of a subconscious desire to see Amanda Stanley rather than get to the bottom of the Derek Sedgwick affair?

No, surely not. Maybe. Life can be pesteringly ambivalent about things like that.

She was still grinning. 'You mustn't think up excuses, Tim. Just come up and see me. Any time.' She patted my cheek like an aunty Mae West and giggled at the joke. 'I mustn't lead you astray, though. Sorry I can't help. I don't know where Derek is, but thanks for warning me that Jerry Foster might come looking. There's not a lot to connect me with bloody Derek these days but you know what the cops are like. I know most of the local ones and they're not a bad lot apart from always wanting me to come to their annual ball, but they do have a habit of leaving all the wrong stones overturned.'

'I know.' I thought of Nobby. 'It's their job, you know. I must be off.'

'Nice to see you, Tim.'

'Same here.' I kissed her cheek. 'Apart from Rossetti marrying here and Holman Hunt at Fairlight, there aren't any other obvious Pre-Raphaelite connections, are there?'

She shook her head. 'Not that I know of. Millais and Winchelsea, of course. And Edward Lear. But not Hastings.'

'Mm. Oh well. Back to the drawing-board. The police think they'll find Derek anyway.'

'Good luck to them.'

''Bye.' I opened the door to another gust of rain. 'Thanks again, Amanda.'

'Any time, Tim. 'Bye. Go carefully. The weather's terrible.'

'You bet.' The door closed and I was back on the pavement in the cold seaside rain, suddenly feeling a long way from home and more than a little bit stupid. What had I hoped to find? Why was I there? I could imagine Sue's face when I told her where I'd been. She'd say I was hopeless, looking for trouble. Visiting the scene of the crime, perhaps, like a poorly motivated hack in an old film of third-rate provenance. I shook myself and made off briskly down the High Street. The scene of the crime; why not visit the cliff at Fairlight?

There was a cut through from the old High Street towards the Bourne where I'd left my car, a sort of alleyway that was half-twitten, half plain alley. Part of it was covered, so, with the rain in mind, I slipped off left into it to keep out of the weather. About ten yards down it opened into a brickyard with an old warehouse wall on one side. It was as I stepped into the yard that the hairs on the back of my neck pricked up at the sound of footfalls behind me, coming up too close, too fast. I turned round, stepping off left to the side of the yard.

The shock was sudden; there were two of them, both Japanese, stocky and low-slung, dressed in grey suits. It was like treading on a pair of ferrets in an empty domestic fowl pen. Surprise and alarm made me spring sideways and throw up my right arm instinctively, which was all to the good because the first one, lower-slung and stockier than the man behind him, was coming in at my ribs, hissing with menace, hand sweeping round to chop at me like an axe-head.

Without even a thought, in the split second available, I gave him the old Wasps Elbow. It was automatic. Habits die hard. My old mate Tubby Postlethwaite used to use the Wasps Elbow and the head-butt without a qualm, which is why he got sent off so often. Tubby played hooker to my tight-head prop and it used to irritate me no end when he got sent off because I'd have to take over as hooker, a position I hated. Nothing but splintered shins, cracked skulls and neck bones out of joint, that's hooking. I should say, quickly, if there are any members of the Wasps Rugby

Football Club reading this, that I never called it the Wasps Elbow myself; that was Tubby's work. Mind you, Tubby was a short, thick, villainous Yorkshireman and he always attributed anything nasty to the South, so that was it, although I suspect that someone from Wasps gave him a deserved black eye once and he was just getting his own back. Tubby was all right to have on your side, but I played against him a few times and we ended up trying to break each other's knees.

However, I digress.

What you do is to fold your forearm back and use the blunt, powerful stub of your upper arm, led by the pointed elbow bone, to punt off your opponent with all the direct force provided by arm and shoulder muscle, using plenty of weight behind it. If the opponent is coming in head-on you could break an elbow joint or put your shoulder out, but the trick is to be moving a shade sideways so that the impact is out of line and you make sure to get your elbow point into his eye-socket.

I gave the Jap the Wasps Elbow just in the nick of time. Smack into his left eye. The hand-chop missed and his head jerked back sharply because he was coming in at me with his weight forward, almost off his feet. Very unpleasant for him. He gave a great hoot of agony and collided with the brick wall, clapping a hand to his peeper.

His mate, who was taller, ran straight into me.

For a moment we flailed about the yard in a tangle of arms and legs while I was conscious of a thump somewhere on the back of my head that made my eyes water. I realized we had hit another wall. For some reason the second Japanese was trying to pin my arms to my sides and, in a moment of clarity, I contrived to stand on his foot. He let go to try and step away and I managed to thump him one before he hit me under the jaw. Then I lost my temper. With the space between us now sufficient I hooked him in the solar plexus, then got a straight jab at his nose. It pushed him back about a foot.

'Pack it up!' I roared at them both. 'Just pack it up! What the hell are you at? Eh?'

They paid no attention. Perhaps they didn't understand. The one with the damaged eye prised himself off his wall and the two of them hurled themselves at me like wildcats. The shorter one couldn't see properly, so I concentrated on the bigger one and for a few crazy seconds it was like a mini-ruck at Cardiff Arms Park, with grunts and thumps and curses and bodies colliding by mistake. Then there was a high-pitched shout and scuffle.

'What's going on there? Police! Someone call the police! Neighbourhood Watch! Where are you?'

That ended it. The short Jap shouted something and the taller Jap shoved me back hard for the last time. Then they scarpered. One minute it was all punches, kicks and curses, the next it was practically silence. Even their shoes must have been rubber-soled. I heard running thuds, then the sound of a car starting. As I pushed myself upright off the wall there was a squeal of tyres from the Bourne end of the twitten and the roar of a car going off fast. I found myself, gasping and dazed, staring at a small knot of old ladies with shopping-trolleys, all gaping at me as I checked a tear on the sleeve of my jacket and wiped a bleeding graze on my knuckles with a reasonably clean handkerchief.

The old ladies didn't look particularly alarmed; I suppose that bikers and World Cup activities have inured your average South Coast town-dweller to the rough and tumble of English seaside excursions.

'Disgraceful,' one of them said indignantly. 'These football hooligans come from everywhere these days.'

CHAPTER 10

The café where we met for breakfast was run by Italians. How Italians have become so adept at providing a really good English breakfast is something best left to Romano-British history, but the fact is that Nobby and I were having excellent bacon, eggs, tomato and mushrooms at a table that looked out through Italian lace curtains on to Victoria Street, whence Nobby would depart, eventually, to Scotland Yard. Sue was not very far from the Tate. I, on the other hand, was a fair distance from work.

'You were attacked,' Nobby said, in his most plonking, hollow, disapproving tone of voice, 'by two Japanese in a side alley in Hastings at about lunch-time yesterday.'

He made it sound like not only a statement but a charge being read out at a County Assize. Sue, who was having a demure croissant and coffee, raised her eyebrows at me.

'That is what I have told you,' I replied, just to re-establish who had been taking the initiative here.

He paused, with his fork in one hand. 'You went to Hastings on the spur of the moment, I think you said?'

'Yes. I did. Say that.'

The fork inserted itself carefully into a piece of mushroom. 'You went to make inquiries about Derek Sedgwick at a gallery in the High Street of the Old Town?'

'That is so.'

He put the mushroom into his mouth, chewed, and spoke after it had cleared the glottis, or whatever. 'It did not occur to you to phone Inspector Foster, who is, after all, somewhat nearer to the locality than you, and advise him that this might be a worthwhile line of inquiry?'

'For heavens' sake, Nobby, stop sounding like something out of an old Edgar Lustgarten film.'

He ignored me. 'You went, specifically and deliberately, despite all the caveats that have been issued, despite the fact that a telephone was presumably at your disposal and you could have phoned this gallery, not to anywhere else but specifically, I repeat, specifically to Hastings. In person. You did not stay in your office at the Bank.'

'Now you are beginning to sound like the lawyer from that play, *One Way Pendulum*. You'll be asking next why it was that I wasn't in Eastbourne, or Newark-on-Trent, or Stoke Poges yesterday, but, by a series of fantastic coincidences, I was in none of these places but—'

'Tim!'

'Sorry, Sue. Yes, I went personally. As I have told you. I went because I thought it would be better to see Amanda Stanley in person. Someone like Foster wouldn't know all the nuances. He'd put his big CID boot right in it. It needed tact.'

A slight frown came to his brow. 'Amanda Stanley? Wasn't there an Amanda Stanley who used to hang around with Sale? Big girl? Blonde?'

'That's my Nobby. The Memory Man himself. Dead right. One and the same.'

He put down his knife and fork. A redder tinge came to the pink freckled face under his ginger hair. 'Good grief. Wasn't that the one at that thrash after the Blackheath match who—'

He stopped. A slight flick of his eye towards Sue quickly corrected itself into a stare at me. His face went solemn again. I became aware that Sue's eyes were resting on me thoughtfully.

'Big girl,' Nobby said, in an absolutely neutral tone of voice. 'Blonde. Dyed hair.'

'Correct.'

'Didn't know you knew her at all well,' he said, voice muffled by a sudden mouthful of bacon, egg, tomato and toast. 'Not at all.'

'I don't, Nobby. I haven't seen Amanda Stanley for a very long time and didn't know her well when I did. But the fact is that she lived with Sedgwick for two years in Maida Vale. Quite a long time ago. And she's not that far from Fairlight. I went to see if there was any reasonable chance of picking up some pointers or other that would cast light on his little game. He's not Amanda Stanley's favourite person by all accounts, so I felt she might be a little more forthcoming to a personal approach.'

'"By all accounts"?' Sue's voice had too neutral a tone to it for safety. 'May one ask where those accounts originated?'

'From a mutual friend of ours who is a Royal Academician.'

She started. 'Really? Who?'

'Sue, I do not think it would be tactful to impart that information.'

She scowled at me intensely for a moment, then her brow cleared. 'Ah. I know who you mean.'

'I hope you've got the right one. We know more than one RA. All married.'

'I'm sure I have.' Her voice had the conviction of personal intuition in such matters that only a woman can evince.

'The fact is, Nobby, that it was a total blank. She's only had a few business dealings with Derek Sedgwick since he went to live in Fairlight and she didn't believe he could handle a painting as important as a Pre-Raphaelite. She certainly doesn't like him and wouldn't have dealt with him if she hadn't needed the cash. There's something deadly about trying to run a gallery like that in that location.' I turned to Sue. 'What was it you said about those people ending up in Hastings? Lack of money, wasn't it?'

She shrugged. 'You'd better not make a thesis out of it, Tim. Or about galleries. Hastings Borough Council might sue you, for one thing, and there are many reasons why people set up galleries.'

'And visit them,' Nobby put in.

She rolled an eye at him. I fixed a stern expression into place. 'There is no need to be offensive, Nobby. Having started, in a manner of speaking, these various strong muscular hares running, I feel a certain responsibility for hunting them down.'

'Very creditable.' His voice was dry. 'There wouldn't perhaps be any other motivation in your pursuit of these honourable aims, would there?'

'Such as?' My voice tightened. We were getting on to thin ice; Sue was looking at him with interest.

'Such as the acquisition, for your fund, of an extremely valuable work of art in circumstances which might redound creditably on yourself?'

'Really, Nobby. I am offended. You know me better than that.'

'Indeed.' The dryness had progressed into the aridity zone. I imagined the malefactors in the dungeons at Scotland Yard, or wherever, dreaded their uncomfortable interviews with Chief Inspector Roberts.

'There's no need to adopt a Presbyterian tone of voice, Nobby. You could hardly expect me to leave things be after the events of the last few days, now could you?'

'Knowing you, no. With any normal, respectable citizen, yes. But it's no good my trying any restraint in that direction.' He sighed and finished his coffee, signalling a waitress for more. 'This is all a digression. You were, you say, attacked by two Japanese, who I am sure you will link with the one found in the wreckage of the cottages.'

'The idea had occurred to me. I'm glad I haven't had to draw your attention to it.'

He ignored that, giving Sue a meaningful look of weary complicity. 'The Japanese gentleman found in the debris was a Mr Taganaki from Osaka. He was a shareholder and very senior member of an industrial company. This will be in today's papers, since identification was completed at Hastings yesterday under the direction of Inspector Foster's inquiry. Mr Taganaki and his companion, one Monica

Haines, were driven to the cottage on Friday evening from Hastings railway station by a taxi whose driver has identified them both. Sedgwick was not with them. Colleagues of Mr Taganaki contacted in London yesterday evening will—' he looked at his watch—'be interviewed by me later this morning. Miss Haines lived in a flat off Kilburn High Road and her family in Stafford has been given the sad news. We are seeking friends or anyone who can trace her movements in the last few days.'

'Well, well done, Nobby. You are getting a shift on. What about Derek Sedgwick?'

His lips pursed themselves. 'Of Sedgwick—' he pronounced the word Sedgwick as would a schoolmaster about to pick up his cane and deliver six of the best to an unfortunate schoolboy of that name—'there is so far very little to report, I regret to say. He was certainly seen in Hastings mid-week. This conflicts—' he rolled an eye at me—'with the statement he apparently made to one Jane Lardner of the Vergam Gallery in Hammersmith in which he said he was off to Spain. That was on the Wednesday or Thursday, she's not sure which. We have checked various airlines and asked the Spanish police in Pamplona to check the property he owns there. Or near there. Nothing so far; but then he can't disappear for long, you know.'

'Oh no. Look at Lord Lucan. Your boys were on him in a trice.'

His mouth set into a line. Sue put a hand on his. I don't know why it is that I can't help baiting Nobby when he's in one of his pompous moods. Perhaps it's because he's usually in one of his pompous moods when I've been caught on the hop and I'm in defensive vein. Freud, or perhaps Jung, might explain these things but by the time one had untangled their explanation the scene would have moved on a few frames and it wouldn't really matter.

'Sheep, goats and soap.' He said the words carefully, as though weighing them up in front of a judge. 'Your contention is that they refer specifically to the paintings of Holman Hunt and Millais?'

'Yes, Nobby. At least, that is how we—Sue and I—interpreted it.'

'Forgive this ignorant ex-member of the Art Fraud Squad, but could you elaborate on what particular significance those clever, intellectual references might convey? Is there something we have all missed? That we should perhaps be concentrating on?'

Never underestimate Nobby Roberts. Never. His eagle eye glinted from one to the other of us, tinged with pink. I half-opened my mouth and then thought better of it. There are some fields that are best left open to Sue; I tread on them at my peril.

'Sheep,' she said clearly, fixing Nobby with a school-marmish stare reminiscent of Mrs Thatcher, 'is quite clearly a reference to Holman Hunt's paintings, particularly *The Hireling Shepherd* and *Strayed Sheep* or, as it was otherwise known, *Our English Coasts. The Hireling Shepherd* was painted near Ewell, in Surrey, where Hunt's uncle owned a farm. The girl in the painting was one Emma Watkins, who worked there. Although the outward depiction is of a shepherd flirting with a girl, a much more serious moral purpose was intended: the shepherd neglecting his flock, like the church was supposed to be doing at the time. There's a lamb on the girl's lap which is eating green apples and so forth. *Strayed Sheep* was painted on the cliff at Fairlight, so the inference from Sedgwick's letter is obvious. The painting was first commissioned as a replica for *The Hireling Shepherd* by a man called Charles Maud but Hunt decided to produce a new picture. It is his most remarkable landscape and since all this started I've looked at it in the Tate. The colours are brilliant. What strikes me as ironic is that it was painted at a place called the Lovers' Seat, a romantic place popular in local engravings which Hunt must have seen. It was only fifteen minutes' walk from Fairlight Lodge, where an artist friend called Martineau lived.'

Nobby swallowed some coffee as she paused and then said, 'Why ironic?' just to show he was listening, like a good boy.

'Why ironic? Because the place where Hunt chose to paint, about thirty feet below the rustic bench that was the Lovers' Seat, has all fallen into the sea; that's what I think of as ironic.'

He blinked. 'You're not thinking that Sedgwick intended this—this clue as a warning of some sort, are you?'

It was my turn to blink. I must admit I hadn't thought of that. It simply hadn't occurred to me that Derek Sedgwick was capable of that degree of premeditation. 'That's a bit subtle,' I said. 'He probably didn't know that.'

They ignored me. 'What about goats?' Nobby seemed to be hooked, now.

'*The Scapegoat* is one of the great images of Victorian Art. You either hate it or you believe it's brilliant. It represents the Talmudic tradition of driving a sacrificial white goat out into the wilderness on the Day of Atonement. A twist of red wool is tied to the goat's horns. If the propitiation is accepted the wool is supposed to turn white.'

'Rather bad luck on the goat, to have to rely on a bit of wool—oh! Sheep again?'

She ignored me. 'The painting is extraordinary in colour. Hunt worked for days on the shore of the Dead Sea to paint the background. While he was painting there the local Arabs nearly killed him. He brought a goat back to England with a load of Dead Sea ooze to paint in his studio for authenticity. He actually had researched, you see, the story from *Leviticus*, and had worked out that the goat was cast out on the shore of the Dead Sea at Oosdoom, so he brought mud and stones back from there. All in eighteen fifty-four.'

Nobby turned to stare out at Victoria Street for a moment. '*And the goat shall bear upon him all their Iniquities unto a Land not inhabited*,' he murmured. 'I know the painting well—it's up at Port Sunlight where we were taken on a course, once. What an image that is; that wretched goat in that horrible landscape. It's too much, isn't it, to think of the analogy being made from those two references—to drop the culprits over a cliff and to run off to the barren north of Spain. Sedgwick couldn't be forecasting that, surely? What about soap—ah, the Lady Lever Art Gallery at Port Sunlight, perhaps? A soap manufacturer's gallery?'

Sue stared at him. 'I hadn't thought of that! I assumed it was Millais, like Tim.'

'Good grief,' I said, 'no one's pinched a painting of Hunt's from Port Sunlight recently, have they?'

Nobby frowned. 'I don't think so. Let's assume not. But it would be unusual for both a Hunt and a Millais to be available at the same time via someone like Sedgwick. Yet his letter to Tim says a couple of, definitely. Anything we haven't thought of about Millais?'

It was Sue's turn to frown. 'I don't think so. When he painted *Bubbles* Millais was simply painting one of his sentimental children blowing soap bubbles. He had no intention of selling it for advertising but Pears Soap bought it and that was that. I mean, it was in the same line as *Cherry Ripe* and *Cinderella* and *My First Sermon* and all that stuff that Whistler hated so much. *The Boyhood of Raleigh* and—What's the matter, Tim?'

'Whistler,' I said. 'Derek Sedgwick said he saw me in *Art News* with a photograph of a Whistler and an Orpen, and a Monet. Whistler hated English subject-painting. I just wondered if the photo in *Art News* sparked off a subtle implication of some sort.'

Nobby sighed. 'This is getting a bit far out, Tim. The soap reference you took automatically to be a Millais. Let's stick to Hunt and possibly Millais and some reference perhaps to Hastings or Fairlight. At least we know that Hunt, who painted sheep and a goat, was at Fairlight.'

'So was Millais,' Sue intervened. 'He and Edward Lear and Hunt walked all the way along the cliffs to Rye. They went down to the beach at Fairlight and Millais found cuttlefish bones washed up. He wanted to take them to

London to use as pounce on his drawing paper. Hunt said he could buy the stuff easily and in any case the Pre-Raphaelites didn't use it.'

'Pounce?'

'Pounce is a fine powder they used to prevent ink from spreading on unsized paper. Well, any sort of dusting powder, even charcoal, used in art. Comes from pumice originally. Anyway, Lear carried the cuttlefish bones for him.' She shivered. 'Cuttlefish bones. That's a grim allusion.'

'And Millais painted there, too?'

'I only know of the Winchelsea thing, the background to *The Blind Girl*. It must have been their next stop after Fairlight on the way to Rye. After what is now called Pett Level.'

'Is it possible that a painting executed by either one of them in that locality could have escaped detection so far? A major painting?'

She shook her head. 'It's very unlikely. I mean, it isn't absolutely impossible, because such finds do occur, but Hunt's output was so painstaking that any major work has been well documented. When he got stuck with *The Scapegoat* for a while he pumped out some easier stuff just to keep alive, but I don't think much has been missed. He painted a couple of other landscapish pieces, one of Fairlight Downs and another of a girl, called *The School Girl*, locally. Lear, who was with him, did *The Mountains of Thermopylae* and the *Quarries of Syracuse*, both at Fairlight quarries.'

'Quarries?' Nobby's voice was sharp.

'Yes. There were quarries at Fairlight. I don't know if there are now.'

'Quarries use dynamite.'

'I don't think,' I intervened, 'that Fairlight quarry is operational in the dynamiting sense any more. Indeed—'

'I'll check it,' he interrupted, looking at his watch again. 'It's probably been first on Foster's list if it's a likely source. I have to go. This has all been a very illuminating, if predictable, experience.' He stood up. 'Until we locate

Sedgwick, we are not going to get too far. And my feeling is that we should not go too far to get him.'

'You think he's here in London?'

'I think so, yes. We are keeping a close watch on Hammersmith. And I think Foster should keep a close watch on Hastings, just in case.'

'Oh dear. Surely not? I can't see Amanda Stanley—' I caught a flash of Sue's eye, and stopped. Nobby leered faintly. I scowled back and his face broke into a sudden grin. He winked at me and left.

Unhelpful beggar.

Sue stood up briskly. 'I shall be late if I don't go,' she said in a voice calculated to put about a thousand miles between me and her. 'Late. Yes. I must go.

'Oh, Sue. Stay. Have another coffee?'

She glared at me. Then she leant forward, just a little, over the table. Not too close. I braced myself; she looked absolutely magnificent but I knew that trouble was imminent. I had, of course, already given her my version of the Hastings excursion but somehow it had come out a bit different from our breakfast conversation. Odd how these things alter in the presence of other people.

'If,' she said, in that same voice, the voice of thousand mile distancing, 'you go off to blondes in Hastings, or Stoke Poges, or anywhere, ever again, without me, I will *slit your throat*.'

Then she was gone; she and Nobby leaving me, as usual, the one furthest from his destination.

And with the bill to pay.

CHAPTER 11

I had a bad morning at the Bank. The breakfast scene
hadn't helped and financial events seemed inconsequential,
irrelevant. The brain teemed with other notions. To be
honest, I hadn't told Nobby and Sue exactly everything
that I'd done in Hastings the day before. They would have
shaken their heads and exchanged significant glances.

From time to time Jeremy popped his head round the
door on some trifling excuse or another, like the movement
of millions of dollars from Brazil or the purchase of a block
of shares for someone. I responded mechanically. My mind
was far away on a cold, wind-blown headland with a squall
of rain sluicing the grass and the muddy path I had followed.

After a ruck in a back alley there's nothing clears the
head like a brisk walk over exposed moors on a cold, wet
day. I had driven up from Hastings Old Town through Ore
and out to Fairlight, where I turned off and headed down
country lanes until I had to abandon the car and, taking a
thick waterproof coat and my tweed rugby-match-watching
cap out of the boot, I had padded up and headed over
footpaths to the bluffs above Ecclesbourne Glen. It's a
shamefaced thing to admit but I'm very susceptible to place
and atmosphere. I wanted to find the spot where Holman
Hunt had painted *Strayed Sheep* and see if it told me anything.
It wasn't more than about half a mile or so from Sedgwick's
smashed cottage and something said to me that Sedgwick
must have been there and thought about it and planned
something, something that involved me and a fraud or a
deal or a swindle of some sort. It had been a relief to stretch
my legs, even in that weather, and feel wind and rain on
my face and see distances you don't see in London, distances
across fields and scrub, valley and headland, out to the
shining, turbulent sea with hefty mist-rain in the Channel

blotting out a distant horizon or maybe, on a clear day, the French coast. I was out on the last promontory before the east of England comes to an end at Folkestone and Dover, up on a ridge with Rye Bay sweeping to my left and, to my right, beyond the blocking swell of East Hill, the view over Hastings to Eastbourne and Beachy Head. It was heady stuff, exhilarating, just the ticket to clear the mind from the events down in the choked old High Street, our of sight, where the two Japs had had a go at me.

Hunt must have had stamina. To walk down that valley every day, I mean, and set up painting opposite the cliffs, still completely recognizable, which are the other feature, apart from the sheep, of his painting. He's overdramatized things a bit, of course, and altered the perspective, and some of the vegetation has fallen away, with the cliffs, into the sea, and they've built a house spang at the top and there's a caravan park behind that, but—but who can complain? I was standing, after about fifteen vigorous minutes, more or less above the spot where Hunt set himself up and I could recognize most of it, which is more than you can say for the majority of nineteenth-century painters' views these days. The rain trickled down my face and my trouser-ends were wet but somehow I felt elated, as though my mind was clearing, not just from the bang the Jap had given me but from the events of the past two days and my feelings about Derek Sedgwick, that rotten painter and desperate trader whom I had really hardly known, yet who had imposed himself upon my life, exploded himself into it, so violently.

Hunt must have had stamina. I know: I've said that. But he must, and so must Lear and Millais if they walked from Fairlight to Rye by lunch-time. I remembered that Hunt had experienced weather just like mine and that one day, when the mist was so thick he couldn't paint, he was accosted by another artist who advised him that the Pre-Raphaelites were all charlatans who painted indoors. Hunt never let on, which made me think rather more favourably about Hunt than Jeremy might have liked. He didn't finish his painting until November and here was I, one November 138 years later, standing where he'd painted it and wondering what Derek Sedgwick had been hatching and why it went so wrong, which is what it must have done.

Sheep, goats and soap. Nobby was obviously concentrating on that too, or at least was prepared to for a while. Sedgwick had banked on that phrase to draw me down to visit him, had planned for me to arrive, had had my note— or had he? My note was, if it had arrived, somewhere in the smashed remains of Lark's Farm Cottages, being sifted through by Foster's forensic team. If it had arrived. Supposing it hadn't? Supposing Sedgwick didn't know what day I would arrive?

Suppose he didn't care? Suppose the deal was all set to go to the Jap anyway and I was being used simply as bidding-fodder, someone to push up the price or accelerate the conclusion of the contract?

Then why blow the customer and the girl off the cliff?

Why kill the garage man?

Standing there on the edge of the headland, I decided that there was no Holman Hunt painting involved in this. I knew it. Don't ask me why: I just knew it. If you want a logical explanation, put it down to my conviction that anyone who took the trouble to paint the way Hunt did, so painstaking, so hardworking, so honest to himself and his work, couldn't have stray canvases still unaccounted for. And no one in his right mind was going to try to produce fake Holman Hunts. The chances of Sedgwick turning up, by some fantastic stroke of fortune, a major work by Holman Hunt was too remote to consider.

Besides, Hunt never referred to that painting as *Strayed Sheep*. He always, always called it *Our English Coasts*. So why write that to me? I got up in my office at the Bank and sifted through the catalogues, books and magazines on the shelves. I could have told Nobby there'd be no dynamite at Fairlight quarry: it hadn't been a quarry for donkey's years. It's a picnic area now, behind Fairlight Church. And Sue seemed to have neglected to mention that Millais didn't start painting *The Blind Girl* until 1854, two years after his visit; he finished it in Scotland. Somehow both Hunt and Millais were slipping out of my mind and I couldn't reconcile that as I got out the back numbers of *Art News* and found the one the Bank's PR department had marked for me, the one with the photo that Sedgwick claimed to have come across that started the whole thing.

There I was, smiling broadly, not 'grinning like a chimp' and there were the paintings, an Orpen, a Monet and a Whistler. In the background you could also see the little terra-cotta figure of Gwen John by Rodin that we'd got from France. I looked at the photo intently and analysed each artwork, one by one.

Whistler: On my way back from Fairlight, over the ridge, I'd passed within two hundred yards of the gravestone of Anna Mathilda McNeil Whistler, his mother, that severe black-clad lady whose portrait was in the Louvre for so long and is now at the Quai d'Orsai or whatever. Whistler was the reason I'd been to Hastings the last time and it hadn't done me too much good then. I'd shivered as I'd driven past Whistler's mother in Hastings Cemetery, but this wasn't about Whistler.

Monet: He was out of it. No connection with Hastings at all.

Orpen: That was a super painting. His blonde model and mistress, Yvonne Aubicq, in the studio, nude, with a still life. I'd paid money for that painting at the time I bought it for the Bank, twenty-seven thousand plus at a time when Orpens were still available at seven or eight grand, not as good as this but still available. Well, the laugh was on my face now. Sotheby's sold Orpen's nude study of Yvonne in bed at breakfast-time, *Early Morning*, for over three hundred grand this year. Jeremy nearly had kittens when the auction price went up. Bought the best champagne and made Geoffrey drink it as well as me. If I'd bought a Van Gogh for a fiver at the local jumble sale he couldn't have been better pleased.

Orpen.

I frowned at the photo. There was something Sue had said about Hastings, something in the car, that made me peer harder at the photograph, where I beamed out at myself like an idiot boy having his first prize at School Speech Day.

Orpen?

The door whipped open and it was Jeremy again. His face was alert, his blond hair glowed. He ogled me suggestively. 'Lunch?' he queried, having evidently failed to arrest a number of suitable clients and transport them to a favourite watering-hole.

'Um, yes, thanks, Jeremy.' Orpen?

'Penny for them, Tim.' He came further into my office. 'You look thoroughly preoccupied, my dear boy. Don't tell me: it will be this wretched Sedgwick business. I do wish you'd put it out of your mind. Although I have to admit that your general *tone* seems much improved.'

Tone? My mind clicked a cog. What was it Whistler had said to Augustus John about Gwen? 'Character? What's character? It's *tone* that matters. Your sister shows a sense of tone.'

Of course! Of course! Knewstub! Jack Knewstub! Sue had said it in the car! When she was talking about the reason Sedgwick squatted on the cliff edge and about the people who'd drifted down to Hastings for reasons of financial failure. That was it!

The phone shrilled, blocking my thoughts. 'Damn!' I shouted at it. 'Not now!'

Jeremy's eyebrow cocked up. The phone rang again. I wrenched it off the hook.

'Two Japanese gentlemen,' my secretary said, before I had a chance to shout at her, 'are here to see you. Urgent, they say. They apologize for not having an appointment. They specifically ask for you. Won't see anyone else. They are from the Taganoshaganaki Corporation. One is the vice-president. Mr Okanura.'

'Japanese? Taganoshaganaki Corporation? The vice-president? Okanura?'

Jeremy's eyebrow had cocked up higher than that of a parrot confronted by a peanut. I put my hand over the receiver. 'Japanese,' I said tersely. 'Probably art business. Er, Sedgwick. I haven't had time to tell you about an, um, an unpleasant, um, incident—' I broke off; his eyebrow had disappeared into his hairline, which is not low. 'Send them up,' I said, hastily; there might be safety in numbers. We were, after all, in our own Bank.

'My dear Tim!' Jeremy's whisper was of penetrating, sibilant pitch. 'What on earth? Incident? Unpleasant? What kind of incident, for heaven's sake? The Taganoshaganaki Corporation is *enormous*. Very prestigious. They're handled by—'

'This way, gentlemen.' My secretary can be far too prompt sometimes. 'Mr Simpson will see you in his office, here. Mr Okanura of the Taganoshaganaki Corporation. Mr Simpson and, er, Mr White. Gentlemen.' She popped out, smartly ignoring her failure to introduce the second man, whose name was probably too difficult. Jeremy, recovering sharply as befitted a City man, had drawn himself up to his full majestic height. I goggled at the spectacle in front of me.

The first man, Mr Okanura, was extremely sleek. Silver-grey threads ran through his superbly smooth, thick hair. His suiting put even Jeremy's to shame. He stepped forward smartly and bowed.

'Please forgive this intrusion,' he said. 'Have come to offer our most humble apology for unwarranted attack. Disgraceful affair. We wish to make amends in any way possible. This gentleman, Mr Taganaki, will apologize.'

He turned and with an expression in which some distaste was carefully revealed, indicated the second man. I was still goggling at him. There's no doubt, you know, that the

Wasps Elbow is ideal for coping with someone shorter than yourself. The second man's left eye, swollen and blackened, was developing into a shiner that Tubby Postlethwaite himself would have been proud of.

'My colleague—' Mr Okanura actually spoke quite well—'made the mistake of believing you responsible for Mr Taganaki's death. He is a cousin of Mr Taganaki's. Serious mistake. Most unfortunate. You have the unreserved apology of me personally and my Corporation. Mr Taganaki will now apologize.'

'Oh, I say—look here—no need—simple mistake. I'm sure—' I saw that Jeremy's face was a picture. His jaw had dropped at least an inch. But there was no restraining Mr Taganaki: he stammered out how sorry he was in florid terms until, writhing, we all knew it was more than enough. He would have gone on forever had Jeremy fortunately not roused himself and boomed an interruption.

'Thank you!' he hollered. 'Thank you! Your apology is accepted. Absolutely! Without reservation. On behalf of both my Bank and Mr Simpson here—' he cast an eye which revealed a good deal of white in my direction—'who, as I am sure you can see, is entirely *unscathed* by the incident. Consider it forgotten. Entirely forgotten. We all make mistakes.'

And blow me if he and Okanura didn't actually bow to each other in true Oriental fashion.

Nobby, I thought, the Japs have been talking to Nobby. That's why they're here and how they know I'm not to blame.

'Most unfortunate,' Okanura said again. 'Glad that all settled. We would now like to discuss a business matter.'

'But of course!' Jeremy was agog. I could see, in his face, the handling of some of the Taganoshaganaki billions. 'Would you care to sit down?'

Mr Okanura remained standing. 'Discussion with Mr Simpson,' he said, moving his gaze from Jeremy to me.

'I beg your pardon?' Jeremy's voice rose slightly above

the level an urbane director of a merchant bank should use.

Okanura stepped towards me. He bowed. 'Famous Mr Simpson. Art investment specialist. Internationally well known.'

'Oh. Oh no, really. I, er, um, think you must be—'

'No. I know. Tim Simpson. Very famous in art world. Mr Simpson, please, I would like to discuss with you.'

'Well—I mean—of course—but what?'

'Painting. My Corporation is willing to give you very high price. I congratulate you.'

'Me? Painting? What painting?'

Mr Okanura smiled, the broad, meaning smile of a man in the know, a man preparing for an enjoyable negotiation. 'I understand your Art Fund must be very keen on this painting. Does not have a Pre-Raphaelite. But it is an investment fund, for profit. We will give you a handsome profit.'

'Pre-Raphaelite?' It was my turn for the pitch of voice to go astray. 'Which Pre-Raphaelite?'

Mr Okanura smiled waggishly. Mr Taganaki of the black eye also managed a crooked grin.

'Rossetti,' said Mr Okanura. 'We wish to buy the Rossetti. A board decision taken. Must be implemented. Very important.'

'Rossetti? *Rossetti?*'

Mr Okanura smiled again the smile of a man who is enjoying the cunning of his opponents in negotiation. 'Of course,' he said. 'Rossetti. *Proserpine?*'

There was a silence. I'm not sure that my mouth wasn't open a lot wider than my boss's.

Jeremy was the first to find his voice. 'I think,' he said, rather hoarsely, moving proprietorially towards Mr Okanura, 'that, since you are guests in our country, we must insist—absolutely insist—that we continue this discussion over lunch.'

CHAPTER 12

'A Rossetti. Rossetti! And he's sold the bloody thing before we've even got it!'

'I do wish,' Sue said, 'you wouldn't pace up and down like that. It's terribly unnerving and I'm trying to think.'

Over the mantelpiece my big Clarkson Stanfield marine painting swirled its sea-green waves capped by foam below the great hulk of a sailing ship, a man-of-war, beating out of the Medway into the Thames. Around the walls various lady artists of Sue's, Laura Knight and Dod Proctor, Sylvia Gosse and Elizabeth Stanhope Forbes, provided gentle or acerbic visions of aspects of life seen through female eyes. My etching of Dorelia by Augustus John showed her fixing that bandanna she wore over her head, arms uplifted to emphasize the femininity of the figure draped by the loose clothes and waist-shawl that became the fashion for girl art students for a couple of generations. Outside, the rain beat down on Onslow Gardens. We were at home.

Sue's distant manner of the breakfast meeting had disappeared. As soon as I'd got home she'd known from my excitement that something was up. It wasn't as though her manner had persisted, anyway; I could tell, when I came in through the door, that the irritation of the morning had given way to some other consideration, something she'd been thinking about during the day. Now my revelations had added another source of distraction. She was deeply involved in everything I'd told her.

'I knew he'd never accept a Pre-Raphaelite into the Fund if he could avoid it. So what does Jeremy do? Takes the Japs out for the best lunch money can buy, fawns all over them, extols the Bank's virtues to them as a London collaborator and then virtually dangles the Rossetti in front of them as bait. Just like a tart sliding a leg out of a short skirt.'

Sue cast a disapproving eye at me. 'You mean he promised to sell them the Rossetti provided they put some of their business the Bank's way?'

'Not in so many words. Of course not. But it was there, underlying everything he said. Future collaboration of mutual benefit, if—mark that if—if we were to have a closer relationship; the development of joint interests; various portfolios of which one, supervised by Tim here himself, of course, might be an art investment one; and so on and so forth. The Japs got the message all right. Okanura's smile got broader and broader as Jeremy went on. He knew.'

'Well, did he promise anything?'

'Of course not. Made a lot of generalized, mollifying set statements in which no firm commitment could be discerned. He's no fool. We have to be as competitive as anyone else.'

'But what about the Rossetti? What did they say?'

'They said that the dead Mr Taganaki was negotiating with Derek Sedgwick for an important Rossetti painting, a full oil, depicting Proserpine. They were being very cautious, especially after that lot from Amsterdam came back and announced that thirty of the Van Goghs in Japan are rank fakes. They're dead keen on Rossetti and Burne-Jones, which made Jeremy wince like a man with toothache biting on a treacle toffee. They knew their stuff, though. Apparently Rossetti painted about eight versions of *Proserpine*.'

'He did. It was one of his favourite images. For good reason.'

'Eh? Who was Proserpine, anyway? Another languishing female?'

She gave me one of her looks. One of those looks you bestow upon a man not only uneducated in any of the classic senses but also one whose masculine insensitivity tramples on images of feminine tenderness and suffering. 'Proserpine, my dearest Tim, was the lady condemned to spend half of the year in hell with Pluto—' she rolled an eye at me—'the god of the underworld, presumably subservient to his every wish, and who lost her true love, Adonis, who died young. Adonis? You remember Adonis?'

'Only in connection with Venus. Pomegranates?'

'Pomegranates?'

'I seem to recollect that Proserpine ate a pomegranate she wasn't supposed to eat. For each seed she consumed she had to spend a month in hell. She's eating one in the painting. I've just remembered.'

'Well done! Absolutely right! Rossetti is said never to have completed the painting to his satisfaction. The subject was deeply significant to Rossetti and his triangle with William and Jane Morris. Jane Morris is, of course, the model. When he struggled with his painting, Rossetti was already very ill, swilling down chloral with whisky, and must have known he didn't have long. So that's how he saw the situation: Jane obliged to live with her husband but adoring Rossetti, her lover, eternally, long after his early death. Her own life, of course, continuing as a form of death in life.'

'Ha! Very convenient. Amazing how we fit our life-situations into self-tailored fantasies. I seem to recall that she was pretty fed up with him by the time he snuffed it and it didn't take her long to fall into the ever-ready arms of that automatic adulterer, Wilfred Scawen Blunt. A man programmed to seduce.'

Sue gave me another old-fashioned look. 'You have the wrong sort of memory for art matters, Tim. Enough of this. Where is the Rossetti? What did the Japanese say?'

'Ah, well, there's the rub, you see. Jeremy was flashing warning glances at me like a lighthouse. We couldn't let on that we hadn't actually got it. And we had to listen to their version of the death of Mr Taganaki's cousin, a version nothing like the one I've been given by Nobby, which was in pure confidence so I couldn't let on about that either. They think that Derek Sedgwick—originally they thought it was me—lured their colleague to the cottage and arranged for its destruction with him in it due to some unspecified skulduggery over money as well as the disposal of the Rossetti. They had been told that I was after the painting—Jeremy was quite right, Sedgwick used my letter as a negotiating ploy—so they assumed I'd got it.'

'How on earth did you get over that problem?'

'Oh, Jeremy was typical. Just a short number of formalities, he said, before we had possession of the work. Matter of ownership. I could've pasted him one! It's typical of the more fly-by-night side of his character, the gambler that lies within everyone like him. He justifies it by what he'll call the downside risk; if we don't get the painting we've lost nothing, we just make excuses, but if we do then there's an immediate profit. It suits him, of course; he's never liked Pre-Raphaelites and he'll be only too glad to move this one on quickly. Now the pressure'll be on me to find the bloody thing, especially if the Bank stands to get good international business from it, quite apart from the Art Fund.'

'Some pressure!' Sue stared at me in indignation. 'Some downside risk! Three people murdered. God knows how close we were to it at that garage. And Jeremy expects you to carry on regardless?'

'Oh, Jeremy won't actually demand as much, he daren't, but he'll flash an eye and quirk his mouth and refer to intrepid incidents of mine in the past and hint and insinuate and ask how Nobby Roberts is getting on with Inspector Foster and—Ah! I've something to tell you. I thought about Hastings—Foster's name has brought it all back. I—'

'Wait! Wait!' Sue stopped me excitedly. 'So have I! I'm sure it's the key! I've got it!'

'What?' I was bursting to tell her, but her face had lit up, her eyes sparkled and she was so obviously mad keen that it would have been unkind to stop her.

'Do you remember? When we were driving around Hastings? No, when we were sitting in the car after the imbroglio at the cliff edge? I said to you that people went to Hastings because it was cheap? Remember?' Sue leant forward, close to me, her face suffused, excited. 'I said that Jack Knewstub, after the affair at the Chenil Gallery with the Johns, retired hurt to Hastings?'

Splendid wife! Oh, dear Sue! How could I stop her, now? She was in full spate, and I knew what she was going to say.

'Guess what? It hit me this afternoon at the Tate! Knewstub's father, Walter John Knewstub, was Rossetti's assistant. It had to be a Rossetti, not a Hunt or Millais. The connection is a straight line. Knewstub—the father—helped to prepare Rossetti's paintings, drew them up, everything. When Jack Knewstub went down to Hastings he might have carried an inheritance with him! What about that?'

I embraced her so hard she gasped out loud. 'You did it! You clever girl! You did it! It was you who hit on it. In the car, when we were at Fairlight. By instinct. That's what Sedgwick's claimed to have found. A Rossetti, not a Hunt or Millais. But he put sheep, goats and soap to throw me off the scent. He was dangling a Rossetti in front of Japs and he had a story, a good solid story, all prepared for them.' I squeezed her again. 'He probably lined up a provenance for his painting to allay their fears about forgeries. I can imagine how convincing he was. I wonder if it really is genuine; the painting, I mean.'

She stared at me. 'It would be very difficult to forge.'

'But not impossible. And there was I, standing in the photograph in *Art News* with an Orpen beside me and Gwen John behind. No wonder he trailed a red herring.' I got the magazine out of my briefcase and laid it out in front of her.

She frowned. 'I don't understand.'

'Guess who William Orpen married?'

Her brow cleared. 'Of course! Grace Knewstub. Walter's daughter and Jack's sister.'

'Guess who the other sister, Alice, married?'

She had gone quite still now. 'William Rothenstein. He painted her with Augustus John at Vattetot-sur-Mer. *The*

Doll's House. She married him subsequently. Sir John Rothenstein's mother. I'm a Tate girl, remember?'

I patted her, left her, went to the big bookcase that runs along one wall of our living-room and pulled out the first volume of William Rothenstein's *Men and Memories*. It didn't take me more than thirty seconds to find the reference on page 229 and read it out. '"Knewstub later became Rossetti's assistant, laying in the first stages, and painting duplicates of many of his paintings, both oil and watercolour, which Rossetti himself signed and disposed of." Written by Knewstub's son-in-law.'

She shook her head gently. 'That's incredible. And Jack Knewstub retired to Hastings.'

'It's even better than that! The case that Derek Sedgwick could make, I mean. Look at that photograph; there's me and there's an Orpen—connection with the Knewstubs immediately—and there's Gwen John, Augustus's sister. John was said to be so angry after the failure of the Chenil Gallery, which Jack Knewstub managed, that he never spoke to Knewstub again. There's an implication that Gwen was never paid some money owing from the gallery and that really riled John.' I got up again and took from the bookcase Michael Holroyd's *Life of Augustus John*. It took me no time to look up the reference to Jack 'Curly' Knewstub.

'His father had been both pupil and assistant to Rossetti—old Knewstub, it was said, could draw but not colour, and Rossetti, a superb colourist, could not draw: it was an ideal partnership.'

She moved her lips into the position of a soft whistle. 'I seem to remember, though, that according to Holroyd, Jack Knewstub was ruined. His family shunned him and he ended up in Hastings with a canary and a kettle for company. He'd modelled himself on John, had lots of children just like him, and then said he was betrayed. He'd hardly be holding on to a Rossetti his father had passed on in those circumstances, would he? Although I suppose there's a final, bottom limit for everyone.'

I put the Holroyd down and smiled at her happily. 'The kettle and the canary is a good story. And the idea of a ruined man in penury at Hastings makes excellent drama in a biography. But in reality he was supported by Orpen a good deal. Orpen's daughter, Kit Orpen Casey, wrote that her Uncle Jack was helped enormously by her mother who, as his sister, was a bit embarrassed to ask Orpen for financial assistance for Knewstub, especially when husband and wife weren't on very good terms. Kit Orpen also had various small treasures left to her by Knewstub; he was her favourite uncle. During the war, the Second World War, he sent the Orpen family delicious parcels in spite of rationing, because he was a brilliant under-the-counter man—steak, butter, ducks, whisky—so it doesn't present quite the picture of destitution one might think. And if he was a brilliant under-the-counter man he'd know the value of things. He wouldn't part with a Rossetti unless there was good cause. If he had been declared bankrupt, all the more reason to conceal any private asset he had. You see: Sedgwick could build up a case that the Japs might find very convincing. All he had to do was to establish that the painting was removed from Knewstub's lodgings at about the time of his death, or at least to hint at some reason why the family didn't get it—perhaps a debt settled or a lady obliged— and the fish would be hooked.'

She swallowed. 'Then why kill the Japanese man? And the girl? And the garage man? What "skulduggery" was going on?'

I got up and put the books back on to the shelves. The books had served their purpose. The research bit was over.

'Until we find Derek Sedgwick and the painting,' I said, 'none of those questions can be answered.'

CHAPTER 13

'He's not in Spain.' Nobby Roberts waved a bit of paper at me as though the printed words were tangible evidence. 'He's definitely not in Spain. Thanks to modern European cooperation and the change in law differences between Britain and Spain, we obtain a very good collaboration from the Spanish authorities now. The Guardia Civil have toiled up the mountainsides of Navarra—in their Land-Rover, I assume—to the address given by one Jane Lardner and which they confirm is indeed an ex-stable being converted, sporadically, by one Englishman named Sedgwick, an artist, who visits from time to time. He is not there now. He is not anywhere in that neighbourhood now. He has not been seen there for one month. The last time he was seen there, one month ago, he was ordering some stone for the building walls from the—' he consulted the piece of paper—'Compañía Navarresa de Piedras y Arenas, which means the Navarra Stone and Sand Company, who have—' he paused, now, for effect—'a quarry in that vicinity.'

'A quarry?'

'A quarry. Northern Navarra has many stone quarries. It is, in case your geography has temporarily eluded you, in the foothills of the Pyrenees. Stone is quarried there. By drilling and blasting. With dynamite. The owner of the quarry has helped Sedgwick with supplies of stone for restoration and has, indeed, been seen drinking with Sedgwick in a local bar. He does not deny it, of course, because he says there is no reason why he should. There is no law against his having a drink with an English customer.'

'Indeed not. Quite right.'

'He has never, of course, according to him, allowed dynamite out of his premises. Especially not to customers.'

'No. Well, he wouldn't, would he?'

'No. He wouldn't.'

'So there we are. There is no evidence to suggest that Sedgwick was, or ever has been, in the possession of dynamite.'

'There are days—' Nobby Roberts's teeth were beginning to meet in a manner I can only describe as savage—'when I think that a blow between the eyes with a hammer would do you a power of good.'

'Don't tell me—this is one of them?'

'How did you guess?'

I grinned at him. We were having ploughman's lunches in a pub just off Trafalgar Square called the Doctor Watson, a title to which Nobby particularly takes offence but a pub which serves an excellent ploughman's and a good bitter beer. It is also very convenient for him to nip out of Scotland Yard, round the corner from Broadway into Victoria Street, and meet me. It is not convenient for me at all but, as you will have gathered, I am an obliging bloke in many respects. The fact that those who work in the City of London, like Jeremy, regard Trafalgar Square as about four days by mule train from Bishopsgate or Lombard Street is to their disadvantage. I am quite happy to nip along from the City to the West End because I find the latter as cheerfully spendthrift as the former is chronically stingy.

'You are determined to nail Derek Sedgwick for this matter, Nobby, regardless of the facts. What will you do if he shows up tomorrow, all amazement and good-heavens-me, having been returning from Spain overland, taking his time to paint the odd canvas or two?'

'It says here he hasn't been seen for a month!'

'That doesn't mean he hasn't been to Spain.'

He actually ground his teeth. 'What about his letter to you? Eh?'

'Ah. Now that does need an explanation. It does not, however, put a stick of dynamite in his pocket.'

'All right. All right. *When* he turns up and *when* we get an explanation, we'll decide whether it will hold water or not.

In the meantime I can tell you that we have searched the premises of the Vergam Gallery from top to bottom and he's not there.'

'You searched the Vergam? With a warrant? I bet that upset Jane Lardner.'

'It did. But we turned up nothing. Once we had established that he was not in Spain at the address she gave us, then we could legitimately search. That American from New Orleans is still there. Well established, I'd say. He claims he's going to take some of those paintings back with him. He seems to think they're good. I must say they were quite different from what I imagined Derek Sedgwick would paint. I'm no expert, of course, but they seem very well drawn.'

'I'm no expert either. I don't much like that sort of stuff. Too bright. But anyway, that's not important. Sedgwick has tried all sorts of styles to see if he could hit the target, so far without great success. What is important is that he may just have stumbled on a real Rossetti via the connection I've described to you, something worth a million, perhaps. He was about to sell it to a Japanese corporation whose envoy he was spicing up by his girlfriend's attentions and whose bid he was upping by the use of my name and that letter, when bingo! Off the cliff they go. Why?'

Nobby pursed his lips. Nothing came out of them for a while and then the shadow of a smile came to them. It made me very nervous. When Nobby starts to enjoy himself like that it means you are going to get the short end of a situation.

'You are a City man, aren't you?' he murmured. 'I mean, a banker and that? You and Jeremy both?'

'Of course we are. There's no need to gloat like that, Nobby. What should we know that we don't?'

'Well, far be it from me, of course, a simple policeman, to teach you high financiers your business. I mean, I'm only a humble member of the Fraud Squad with some art experience. But you may have noticed, in the papers recently, that Japan has been experiencing a series of scandals.

Mostly to do with politicians and bribery. I'm not saying your Mr Okanura is connected with the ones you've read about. But I think you may find that there was more than a simple purchase going on. We have had a whisper, through sources that I can't reveal, that a few of these art purchases, not the ones at public auction, have had certain aspects to them which were fraudulent. To do with over-invoicing, I believe. In these days of record pricing for everything, double your money, know what I mean, who can establish the real price paid for things? Maybe your Mr Taganaki got greedy. Maybe his arrangements became a threat. The role of Monica Haines is the key to the conundrum.' He finished his beer. 'I'm sure of that. Otherwise why would she be blown over the edge? And why are the other ladies in the case so vitriolic about her? I must be off.'

'Hey, hang on, Nobby! What is this about Monica Haines?'

He stood up. 'I'm afraid I'm not the expert in that direction. Foster, down at Hastings, is. You'd best speak to him about that.'

'Nobby!'

'It would be quite unethical for me to pass on the results of the case officer's inquiries. Absolutely unethical. It must be his decision whether to impart such information to outsiders and whether it would assist his case or prejudice it.'

'Nobby! For Christ's sake! You're not going to make me fag all the way back down to Hastings again?'

He leered at me. 'Didn't think you'd object to going down to Hastings. In fact, I thought you were looking for an excuse. You see, I remember the Sale Rugby Club vividly. Especially its changing-rooms.'

CHAPTER 14

Inspector Foster pushed his glass of beer slightly away from him, leant back in his chair and stared briefly out of the window across the promenade to where the English Channel was heaving itself, grey and white and broken, into a spray-whipped jumble of thunderous movement along the shingle of Hastings beach. Away to our right the pier braced itself against the heavy thumps of the attacking sea. Signs danced in the wind. Only the occasional human figure, wrapped against the weather, moved cautiously along the wet paving of the raised wide walk by the water, keeping away from the railings at the edge where, now and then, a huge vertical plume of spray seemed to poise itself before exploding across the promenade and on to the road. Sue looked out, shivered, and averted her gaze.

'That's a complex sequence,' Foster said, as though thinking deeply. 'Very complex, for a non-art man like me.'

Non-art might have been a very appropriate adjective for Foster. He was crisply clean-shaven and barbered, dressed in a well-used suit and blue shirt. I put him at around thirty-six, perhaps a bit younger. There was an atmosphere of practical application about Foster, something workman-like and technical that might have indicated an engineer except for the shrewd look at human beings, of interest in them, that surfaced from time to time as he glanced round the pub's saloon bar.

'I realize that,' I said. 'It took us a bit of time to work it through, as well. But it's a theory that fits, so we thought it might be worth applying. I mean, the theory's not much good without some legwork to back it up.'

Foster nodded absently, finished his beer and raised his eyebrows at me in what I took to be an offer of a return drink. Sue shook her head and placed a hand over her glass.

I reflected that Foster was different from other CID men
I'd known in that he drank beer instead of the hard stuff,
but this was lunch-time and he might have a personal rule
about it. He came back from the bar and put a glass in front
of me, nodding briefly at my thanks. Then he looked out of
the window at the racing grey scud for a moment before
turning back to us both, to speak.

'I like the theory,' he said. 'This man Knewstub and all
that. But a policeman's life is full of practicalities, not art
theories. They won't arrest anyone. I'm not really concerned, I'm sorry to say, with how some painting or another
came maybe to be the cause of a crime or even actually the
cause of a crime. History doesn't arrest criminals. The facts
of this situation are simple yet maddening. This business
should have been wrapped up within two days. First, we
have a crime at that cottage. It has been conclusively proved
that a small charge was placed under the cliff, causing the
fall. The two deaths thus rank as murders. Forensic evidence
proves that. Then there is the garage man, Bengate. Death
due to a blow on the head, not with a blunt instrument but
almost certainly a human blow of great force, with a fist.
Bengate had a thin skull and was old. He was probably
killed by the hæmorrhage resulting from the blow. This
could be murder or manslaughter.'

He paused for a moment, drank a sip of beer and sighed
a slight sigh before continuing. Sue cocked her head a little
to one side, showing a restraint that was uncharacteristic.

Foster looked at me. 'Within a short space of your first
visit to the garage, someone went there, hit the garage man
and removed the Morris Minor 1000 that you had noted
in place in the side alley, outside the workshop doors.
Unfortunately no one else saw the Morris Minor, but you
clearly did and I take you to be an extremely reliable
witness. We have asked around locally for witnesses and no
one has come forward, so the only testimony to the existence
of the car is you. Personal considerations apart, I can take
you to be a reliable witness because the reason you went

back to the garage was precisely because that Morris Minor had gone missing. What I cannot establish is whether that car belonged to Sedgwick or whether Sedgwick was involved at all. We have assumed that it was Sedgwick's because we know that Sedgwick had one and there is no sign of it at his cottage or anywhere else. We have therefore assumed that Sedgwick was involved. These are reasonable assumptions but not hard and fast facts; we have to be prepared to modify our thinking. What drives me mad is the disappearance of Sedgwick and the car.'

He sighed again and scowled briefly out of the window, the scowl deepening as the scene outside showed just the same lack of organization and order in weather terms as his case from the clifftops at Fairlight.

'The bloody car. As soon as I was called to the garage from the cliff edge and you told me why you'd gone back there, I put out a call to pull in any likely Morris Minor within the area. I calculated that maybe whoever took it had had half an hour to an hour. With these roads and that car we're talking of thirty or forty miles, probably. That's most of East Sussex, and Kent as far over as Folkestone and Dover, depending on which way it went. By all accounts it wasn't in good nick. We stopped all sorts of Minors. All sorts. You said, I remember, it was a lightish colour, probably greyish-blue, and could be rusty around the doors and sills. You'd be amazed how many of those there still are around the south-east of England. We stopped bloody dozens of them. Upset all sorts of people. Not a whisper. Not a breath. There was no sign of that car, or a car like that, with Sedgwick or anyone like him in it. We don't think he crossed over by ferry from Dover because we were searching in time to check that and he'd have been bloody lucky to cross over without detection, to have driven straight on to a ferry that was leaving there and then, to avoid us.'

'On the other hand, he might have dumped the car in a side-street somewhere, or anywhere, and crossed as a foot passenger. He could then have caught a train down to Spain and been in his disused stable, establishing an alibi, within twenty-four hours.'

Foster gave me an old-fashioned look. 'He might have. It had occurred to me. He would be pressed to establish the alibi, even in Spain, pretending he'd been there since mid-week or something, but he could have a go and we'd have a lot of trouble breaking it down. I don't think a side-street is right for dumping the car even though it is unremarkable. We'd come across it eventually, just like Lord Lucan's. I think a lock-up garage is par for that car.'

'A lock-up garage?' Sue leant forward, interested. 'But he'd have to have access to a lock-up garage, previously arranged, to be able to hide the car away in it at a moment's notice, just like that.

Foster smiled. 'Indeed he would. And Mr Sedgwick is just the sort of man to have a lock-up garage somewhere, available to him, for various purposes.'

'Oh?'

The smile widened slightly. 'Now it's my turn to theorize. There's a good dissertation, somewhere, for someone to write on the role of the lock-up garage in modern society. There are hundreds of thousands of lock-up garages in this country, thousands in this area alone. Most of 'em are used to put cars in. You've seen them, rows of them by blocks of flats or down a lane by some allotments, or just the oc-casional single one by a house. In towns like this a lock-up garage is a golden asset because parking has become so difficult and you pay big money to own one. But they're not only used for cars. They are the ideal, anonymous storage facility. Somewhere to put things you can't house or you don't use much or—' he paused for emphasis—'you want to hide. If the locks are good it's a form of large, convenient safe. We are always interested in lock-up garages and the comings and goings around them. Stolen goods can be hidden in lock-up garages. Not the very public garages in view of blocks of flats or even the individual ones where movement is of neighbouring interest, but the anonymous commercial ones in odd rows behind housing estates or near factory estates. The ones where people coming and going don't know each other much and don't particularly care who uses the other garages. There are lots of those. In them, you find the most extraordinary things, quite apart from cars. Antiques and stolen paintings; household goods removed to avoid valuation for probate; stolen TV sets and consumer durables; furs; fashion goods; clothes; illicit things of all kinds; I won't go on. I reckon that if someone did an assessment of what the lock-up garages of Britain contain there'd be shocks for quite a few people.'

'And you think Derek Sedgwick had a lock-up somewhere?'

'I think it's very possible.'

'Near here?'

'It's a likely possibility. He couldn't store much at that poky little cottage and he must have thought about its vulnerability to landslide anyway. It would be stupid to store anything valuable there.'

'But he didn't own much and a lock-up costs money.'

Foster still looked at Sue good-humouredly. 'People acquire lock-up garages in all sorts of ways as well as renting them. He might have got a bit of money sometime and picked one up cheap as an investment. Before all this traffic congestion got really bad, a few years back, they weren't so expensive and a garage here in the Old Town was obviously going to be worth holding on to.'

'So you think he put the car away in a lock-up and went off somewhere?'

'It's a line we've pursued.' Foster's troubled look returned. 'Without success so far, but we will keep going. I don't know if it's registered in someone else's name—the titles to all the lock-ups in Hastings would take more staff than we've got and a computer to analyse. As for the somewhere he went off to: my guess is London, but I have to be open minded. We know he has associations with the Lardner woman's Vergam Gallery. We are keeping a careful eye on that with the collaboration of the Metropolitan Police. Your friend is very helpful. We know that Sedgwick isn't there now.'

I couldn't hold back any longer. 'But none of this explains a motive for murder! You don't bump off your Japanese client. Even if he is having it off with a girlfriend. By all accounts Derek was a broad-minded man in that direction. At least, his own example couldn't impose jealousies of that sort. The garage man looks like a mistake, a wild card. Derek Sedgwick needed the car urgently and the old codger probably tried to stop him taking it. Mind you, I can't envisage Derek having the strength or the fury to do that.'

'People in tight corners do terrible things.'

'He's such a thin, weedy sort of beanpole. Was any money taken from the garage?'

'No. Till and receipts all intact. There was no one in the workshop that morning. Not enough lucrative repair work available to pay the mechanic overtime on Saturday morning. Filling station only.'

He scowled again and his expression took me back to his face, the first time we'd met again, at that cliff edge, harassed and irritable, waving me off. A CID man at a supposed natural disaster that wasn't, going on about drug-taking, knowing nothing, then, about Derek's letter and sheep, goats or soap. I wondered how much he was really prepared to tell me; suddenly I felt that Sue and I and art were only on the fringe of things, a froth on much deeper waters.

'What is it?' Foster asked suddenly, and I realized I had been staring at him much too intently. It was time to see what I could get.

'This is really all about something else, isn't it?'

'Else?'

'Yes.' I pushed my glass away. 'When we arrived at the cottages and you were already there, you were really conducting an investigation into something to do with drug-taking. I reacted badly to that, but to you I might just as well have been another London swinger who was participating in sniffing of some sort. You must have had Derek under observation. Otherwise you'd never have been out at that cottage. Unless—' the thought hit me suddenly—'it was the Japanese you were keeping tabs on?'

Foster shifted uncomfortably. Sue's eyes had widened and she leant forward again. 'Was it?'

'No. At least, not as such.'

'Ah! It was Monica Haines, then?' I had a vision of Foster, when I'd made my statement in the police station, after the garage affair, tamping down the papers and saying there was nothing more we could do, not even identification. He'd known then, of course. He'd known it was Monica Haines and the Japanese in the cottage, not Derek Sedgwick. How long had he known that?

'In a manner of speaking.'

'What manner of speaking?' Sue's voice was quite sharp. Foster glanced quickly at her, putting on a policeman's impassive look. He retreated from his confidential manner instinctively and I felt, for a moment, that we'd get nothing more from him. I underestimated the power of an attractive woman's intense interest; Foster crumbled.

'Monica Haines moved in circles where drug-taking is habitual.' Foster's voice had dropped. 'This is entirely confidential, mind. Some of it is the social sort of cocaine-sniffing; some of it is the milder smoking of marijuana; some of it is very serious heroin-related stuff. We were collaborating with Drugs Squad people in London when we got the news that our own rather provincial and pathetic addicts were starting to get the odd supply from a visitor who was in contact with London sources. Monica Haines. She was, we were told, the girlfriend of one Derek Sedgwick and visited him from time to time, although she lived in London. He was virtually a squatter in a condemned cottage on the cliffs at Fairlight, we were told. In fact, that cottage wasn't condemned. The local council was pressurized to do something about the cliff situation a couple of years back so they shored up the lower section and announced that there was no further danger. No one locally believed them and only an outsider like Sedgwick would live in those cottages because another section of cliff towards Pett Cove fell in six months ago. In fact, the irony is that if we hadn't been suspicious about that cottage fall, everyone would have accepted it as a natural disaster. If Sedgwick's girlfriend hadn't been under suspicion it would have been treated as accidental death and the council would have got a rollicking. As it was, I insisted on a check and forensic found traces of the explosion. Dynamite. Quarry dynamite. Only a small charge, but absolutely effective. When you made your remarks on the cliff edge you were saying out loud suspicions that I vaguely had already. I got a check done and bingo! You were right. Very odd, that was.'

'Good grief. But someone—Derek Sedgwick presumably—must have pre-set that charge in anticipation of something.'

'Not necessarily. According to an army consultant of ours, a captain in the Sappers, anyone with a bit of knowledge could have nipped down that cliff and set the thing off in thirty minutes flat. In the wind and weather that night there wouldn't have been a lot of noise heard in the cottage or in the area when the bang went off. Just a thump.'

'It's incredible. What a way to murder someone.'

'Not so incredible when you think that a cliff collapse might have been accepted by us all.'

'It's still incredible. There must be the most extraordinary plot behind all this. Some incredible plan that we haven't got hold of.'

'Oh no.' Foster finished his beer and shook his head. 'Not if my experience is anything to go by. There are two possibilities in every crime—one, the Master Plan or Conspiracy theory, and two, the Cock-up. It is the Conspiracy that's the rare animal. In nearly every case I've known, most of it has been a cock-up. I'm willing to bet that when we get to the bottom of all this there'll be a wonderful cock-up behind it. Especially from what I've heard about Sedgwick. By the way, since you are a master at the intuitive approach, do you know anything about an American mate of Sedgwick's called Douglas Rostin?'

I shook my head. 'No, sorry, I don't.'

'Douglas?' Sue was quicker. 'We met an American called Doug at the Vergam Gallery with Jane Lardner. From New Orleans?'

'That's him. Most likely.'

'Blond hair, blue eyes, sunburnt?'

'Never seen him.' Foster smiled. 'He's staying at the Vergam Gallery, though; and your description sounds right.'

'It must be him. Don't know him. Why?'

Foster grunted. 'He goes out to phone. You may not think that odd, but he leaves the gallery to make phone calls when there's a perfectly good phone indoors. He goes to a call-box. My Metropolitan Police friends tell me he hasn't left London to their knowledge, although they've lost him a couple of times. The odd thing is that he phones transatlantic numbers from the box using a credit card, but he also makes cash calls. They're untraceable. The Met boys watch his dialling from outside. They couldn't make out the number, in the weather, but they think that one of the calls he made had the 0424 code. That's Hastings.'

'Good heavens. So—so either he's trying to contact Derek Sedgwick down here or Derek Sedgwick's up in London and using this Doug to contact someone for him?'

'Could be. Could be calling someone else, though.'

'Wait a minute— has this Doug called anyone in Spain?'

'We don't know. He might have. But Sedgwick doesn't have a number in Spain.'

'It could be pre-arranged.'

'It could be.' Foster stood up. 'I have to go. Thank you very much for the information about Knewstub and the Rossetti. As you will have gathered, there are more aspects to this affair than your Rossetti, though.' He paused. 'Did you ever know a Mrs Gallagher? An antique shop in George

Street, off the Old Town High Street? About sixty-five, seventy? Grey-haired old bat?'

'No. No, I didn't. I thought they were pretty much junk shops there.'

'They are, most of them, but not all. Sedgwick was seen at her shop from time to time.'

I shook my head. 'Sorry. Means nothing to me. What does she say?'

Foster pulled a face. 'She doesn't say. She died of a heart attack about a month ago.'

'What's the connection?'

Foster shrugged. 'I'm not sure there is one. Just thinking out loud. You didn't come all this way down here just to see me, did you?'

'Principally you, yes. We might pop in to the Old Town while we're here, though.'

Foster grinned. 'I bet I can guess who you'll drop in on.'

'Can you?'

Sue stood up as well. 'Of course he can! Come on! I'm as anxious to meet this blonde bombshell as you are. I might as well see who it is that's got all the men in this area tied up in knots.'

CHAPTER 15

Strangely enough the two girls got on very well. I suppose they had art in common and, well, to a greater or lesser extent, me. In the case of Amanda Stanley it was a very much lesser extent but an extent of some sort, difficult to define and embarrassing to think about in the sense that my motivations were giving me cause for reflection. But she greeted us with enthusiasm, made tea, beamed at Sue, flattered her with remarks about her job at the Tate and said how good one of the exhibitions Sue had organized had been. She was a sight for sore eyes, with her blonde hair piled high and tied in a black bandanna this time, a clinging yellow dress showing off the impressive figure beneath, the long legs encased in dark stockings that somehow made her look sultry. Sue rolled an eye at me at the very first sight of her but soon she and Amanda were chattering their way round the gallery, Sue showing a lot of interest, Amanda pointing out some drawings of her own and a gouache she'd done of the west side of the town with St Clement's Church prominently in the centre. Sue knew the work of one or two of the other artists, the RA and the Cork Street man particularly, so she made intelligent comments about them and peered at the local landscapes and the watercolours and admired the cow in the centre of the floor and some pottery with wavy edges that was set out on a table. We drank the tea and talked art for a bit and how tough the business of having a gallery is. Sue went back and looked at Amanda's work and said she ought to do more herself, she was good, which pleased Amanda and she gave us more tea as the afternoon turned dark and the lights came on outside.

'We've been talking to Inspector Foster,' I said eventually, to keep things open and above board. 'We wanted to test a theory on him. About paintings—Pre-Raphaelite paintings—in Hastings.'

'Jerry Foster? Really? I can't imagine Jerry Foster going in for art theory very much; he's such a practical man.'

'True. But he liked the theory.'

And then I told her all about the Japanese and the Rossetti of Proserpine and how we'd managed to establish a link between Rossetti and Hastings quite outside his marriage at St Clement's or Lizzie Siddall's frequent visits for her health, through Jack Knewstub and his father Walter having been an assistant to Rossetti who actually produced Rossettis—the paintings, that is—after a fashion. Her eyes got rounder and rounder and she began to splutter after a while. Sue just sat and listened, her eyes roaming round the paintings on the walls in a sort of constant scan that I found curious, but I was too busy telling Amanda how clever we'd been and enjoying the rich sight of her to have too much time to think about it or interrupt myself.

'But good grief!' Amanda protested eventually. 'That's just too fantastic! I mean, it's so fantastic that it probably has to be true. I've no idea where Jack Knewstub lived while he was here but I do remember reading somewhere that he came from Manchester like me and was called Curly because of his hair. I think his father was in Manchester to help Ford Madox Brown with his murals, so perhaps that was how the son came to be born there. I've always been interested in gallery exhibitions and particularly the Chenil Galleries because of Orpen and Augustus John. The Chenil, under Jack Knewstub, had Orpen and John and the Ambrose McEvoy of course, the three great portrait painters from the Slade. But Knewstub ran shows for Pryde and William Nicholson and Muirhead. Did you know he introduced John Barbirolli to London concert audiences? Everyone in Manchester knew Barbirolli from the Hallé but it took Knewstub to get him to London. It's a pity he was a great promoter but not a businessman. John behaved very badly to him in the end, but then John behaved badly a lot of the time, especially with women.'

She grimaced rather grandly, expressing a knowledge of men who behaved badly with women that went deep and which I didn't wish to investigate. I had forgotten, in enjoying the sight of Amanda Stanley so much, that she had taught art for so long and that her knowledge ran so wide as well as deep. Like most men confronted with the sight of someone like Amanda Stanley apparently unattached and without a suitable male to keep her company, I suppose I felt a sense of waste, of loss, as does a matchmaking matron confronted with a wealthy and personable bachelor who resists all efforts to lure him into marriage. It was quite irrational, of course; Amanda was as professional as anyone in her own field and was quite capable of looking after herself.

'Speaking of bad behaviour,' I said, to change the subject somewhat, 'I suppose you've heard nothing about Derek Sedgwick?'

She gave me a very old-fashioned look and, out of the corner of my eye, I saw Sue cease her survey of the walls to frown momentarily in what I took to be disapproval.

'No, I haven't,' Amanda said. 'And I don't want to. I suppose it's inevitable that everyone asks me—Jerry Foster's been here asking the same thing, of course—but I think it's very unfair. I only dealt with him from time to time on an as and when basis, not regularly, and I've told you how I feel about him. He was an unpleasant necessity. Quite honestly, I can't imagine how he could have got on to a Rossetti like that, perhaps via this Knewstub connection, but the whole thing's so fantastic that it could just be true. I mean, everything about this business is so over the top that I'm prepared to believe anything, now.'

'Sorry. Very sorry. It was thoughtless of me. I didn't mean to upset you. Of course you can't have heard anything more than we have, which is precious little. He really seems to have disappeared, together with that terrible old car of his. It's extraordinary; until you come across something like this you can't believe it. I mean, when Lord Lucan did a bunk one naturally assumed it was all a set-up, but this is very similar and I'm sure that Derek Sedgwick doesn't have ranks of influential friends who might be able to fix him up with a new identity or something. Foster thinks the car has been secreted somewhere locally and gave us a dissertation on lock-up garages, which they're working their way through, so far without success.'

'Really? Lock-ups?' She stared at me for a moment. 'I suppose that might make sense. It's all right though, Tim, no need to apologize, I'm just a bit sensitive about Derek at present.' She gave me a conciliatory smile. 'To think that Derek might have got his hands on a Rossetti makes my blood boil. I bet he didn't pay anything for it or let on to whoever was selling it what it really was. I expect it was the sort of thing that Knewstub did a black-market swap for during the war—in return for luxury foods, I mean— and the black marketeer didn't have too much idea about it. Not here in Hastings, anyway.' She pulled another rueful face. 'There I go again, running Hastings down. It's you London swells that bring that on.'

'Us? Swells? We live in suburban Brompton, not St James's.'

She grinned broadly. 'Go on with you! City slicker written all over you.'

'Tim.' Sue's voice wasn't sharp or defensive but the note in it was unmistakable to me. 'I'm awfully sorry, Amanda, but we do really have to get back because it'll take us two hours and I have things I must do before tomorrow.'

'Of course! Sorry, me gassing on like that.'

'No, no. It's all Tim's fault. He gets his teeth into some-thing and then he won't let go.'

Amanda Stanley turned to look at me at that, opened her mouth as if to say something, thought better of it, winked at me, and smiled at Sue.

'It's been great to meet you,' she said. 'I'm glad to see

that Tim's under such good management. I'd love to see you again; perhaps we could meet up in London at an exhibition sometime?'

'That would be lovely,' Sue said. 'Please do ring me and we'll go together.'

'Fine.' Amanda Stanley gave me a peck on the cheek, embraced Sue, and in no time at all we were out on the gust-blown pavement, heads down into the dark, freezing squalls. I got ahead of Sue, opened the car, tucked her in, closed her door and was in beside her as fast as possible. Sea-spray and rain swished down the windows, but my tousled wife, her brown hair streaked with damp, was suddenly a wonderful contrast to the exotic artificiality of Amanda Stanley. I took a slim hand in mine and leant across to kiss her rather pale, cold cheek.

'That was a bit sudden,' I said, not starting up the engine. 'Thought you were taking to the gorgeous Amanda rather well. Then the sudden exit.'

'I was.' Sue was staring ahead, her eyes unfocused. They came slowly round to me and concentrated, blue and serious. Under the cardigan that had kept her warm along with a thick tweed half-coat her breathing seemed a little erratic, as though the dash to the car had flustered her. The effect was somehow erotic and I wanted to embrace her but I knew that this was no moment for shenanigans. 'You are a very innocent fellow, sometimes, Tim,' she said quite affectionately, as though she had found me behaving virtuously inside a den of vice.

I kept hold of the slim hand, warming it. 'Me? It's not a day or two ago you were complaining how suspicious I am. You're not suggesting that Amanda's after my fragrant body, are you? Because I can assure you—'

She waved the flippancy away with an impatient gesture. 'No, of course not! I suppose it's unfair of me; you didn't have time to look. And you couldn't be expected to notice, despite all you've picked up about art. You don't see things the way I do.'

'See things? What things?'

'What things?' Her eyes were serious, troubled. 'Those drawings and that gouache of hers.'

'What about them?'

She bit her lip and looked at the spray-stained windscreen before replying.

'Just one thing about them. I'd bet on it. Whoever drew them—and coloured them—is the same person who draws and colours Derek Sedgwick's gouaches at the Vergam Gallery.'

CHAPTER 16

We only drove about four hundred yards before I stopped the car. I chose a spot beside some flat shingle at the back of the fishing area, where the black ribbed structures of net sheds towered like dark monoliths around us. Bits of wet, rusty equipment and empty vehicles stood on the pebbles and weedy litter. It was blowing hard and the car shivered as the gusts struck it. Somewhere ahead surf thundered on the shore, out of sight but ever present, like bad weather trying to get in to a weakened house.

'Either,' I said for the fifth time, 'she is painting his or he is painting hers. Knowing how he used to paint, it must be her throughout.'

I never doubted Sue's judgement. If Sue said that the pictures in Amanda Stanley's gallery were executed by the same artist as Derek Sedgwick's in Hammersmith, then that was good enough for me. Sue is the expert when it comes to that sort of assessment. And it all fitted, it all fitted only too well. Derek Sedgwick had never painted like that, could never paint like that. Those bright colours, the bold, primary attack; a vision of Amanda Stanley came to mind, her clothes, her style, the yellow bananas. It had to be her. And the drawing: as Sue said, the drawing was good, it was trained, it was confident. It was much too good for Derek Sedgwick. Hadn't Nobby Roberts said the same thing? Derek Sedgwick wasn't confident enough for that; his art had been all too derivative, too trendy. Amanda would never be a Van Gogh but she was at least individual, worth appreciating in her own right.

'Why? For God's sake, why?'

'Money,' Sue said unhappily. 'I feel desperately sorry for her. It must be a struggle. It's happened before, you know: one artist passing off another artist's work as his own. In a way it's an understandable marketing ploy; authors often write under different names to create more opportunities for themselves, so why shouldn't artists do the same thing?'

'It's not the same thing. Authors may use pseudonyms but they're still only the one author. Here we have two separate people.'

We were, of course, avoiding the issue. The issue hung around the air inside the car like a vast evil genie of a mythical lamp, waiting to stream forth at the slightest rub. Our minds kept flinching at it. The way we kept dealing with the surface issue of the paintings was like a tennis-player's attention to his shoelaces. The match was yet to be played, the judges were waiting.

'We have to go back,' I said. 'We have to go back and ask her.'

'Must we?' Sue obviously felt, like I did, that almost anything would be better than facing Amanda, having a distressing showdown with her. The fear was of what else would come out, how far it would go. I began to imagine Derek Sedgwick upstairs above Amanda's gallery, occupying the living space, perhaps in her bed, a bony evil now, to be dealt with like a primæval spider needing squashy blows with a primitive weapon. I shook myself; it had to be faced. It had to be faced by me, by us, before anyone else, so that her explanation could be digested carefully. What Sue had seen wasn't evidence, of course; it wouldn't stand up in a court of law. I had another vision of Derek Sedgwick, an occasion somewhere where he'd grinned and said that all art was interior decoration really, particularly in America, and what the hell did it matter who painted it or signed it, if you liked it that was all that mattered. He must have said that often, as everyone connected with art but not of it does from time to time and still doesn't believe it. What I couldn't swallow was the notion that Amanda Stanley had been lying to me all along, that she was deeply involved with Derek in some way and, if she was, she knew about everything that had happened. There I had stood, rabbiting

on about the Rossetti like a prize twerp, expounding our
theory about Knewstub. Amanda Stanley knew all about
Knewstub already; she had even mentioned his black-
market activities. And I, like a real Charlie, had been telling
an art lecturer from Manchester something she'd known for
years.

'Yes, we must.'

Sue shook her head. 'Couldn't we just tell Foster or
Nobby?'

'No. We have to be certain. She'll believe you when you
tell her you've seen Derek's New Orleans stuff and that you
know it's not his. She'd just deny it to Foster. Nobby
wouldn't come himself, he'd delegate it to Foster. I don't
mind Foster but we have to see Amanda first.'

Sue didn't reply to that. She just looked down at her
hands. I got out of the car into the dark winter's wind, to
smell salt, fish and tar. The lights from opposite pavements
produced a sort of half-gloom, half-twilight. People were
shutting up shops and going home from tobacconists',
wrapped up in thick coats that made their shapes bulky as
they bent into the gale. I went round to Sue's side and
opened her door for her because she hadn't moved. She
came out reluctantly and I threw my heavy coat over her,
not just against the keen wind but in hope of sheltering her
from her discovery and its effects. I took her hand and the
two of us walked together over the dirty shingle on to the
pavement and across the road to the start of the old High
Street.

There was a light on in St Clement's Church, one that
threw the big windows into illuminated Gothic arches
against the dark of the stone walls. It showed the high
vaulted interior grandly because it was not too strong a light
and it left shadows all round the edges of things, beyond
the soaring tracery of arches and roof beams, leaving the
outside fringes a mystery of vaguely discernible shapes the
way all religions do.

There was no light on in Amanda's gallery. The whole

front was in darkness as though ashamed of its contents. The sign on the door said Closed. Yet again a Closed sign I thought, fingers of nervous fear going up the side of my windpipe. I stepped off the pavement and peered at the upper windows. They were dark. Worse nervous fears exceeded the chills of the late winter afternoon.

'The back,' I said to Sue tersely. 'We must go round to the back.'

I grabbed her hand and hustled her along the pavement. After three or four more steps we came to a delivery alley at right angles to the street and crunched down it. At the end it opened out into a blessed series of yards going back behind all the shops and houses, with access beyond small brick barns, stables and outhouses towards the modern road along the Bourne, lit by flaring orange lights a hundred or more yards away.

I led Sue along until we came to the back of Amanda's gallery. The area was very much a back yard, with black plastic sacks of rubbish awaiting collection and cardboard boxes of various sizes sagging in wet, weathered heaps. The back of the gallery came out at right angles in a single-storey block of old stables with a hayloft over them. Three pairs of double doors, painted black, were tight closed but a hoarse thrumming behind one of them indicated a power generator or commercial freezer or some industrious activity's mechanical basis. I went up to the back door and rattled the handle. There was no response from within. We stood together for a moment, undecided, hearing the sound of the town burbling round us, strangely distant from that enclosed back space where only the throbbing generator inside one of the stables provided any close noise. I hammered on the door.

'Amanda?' I shouted.

There was no reply. Suddenly angry, I turned the loose knob and threw the door open, inwards. It gave on to a scullery from which a kitchen led off into the building and I went through it sharply, knocking my hip on a side cupboard irritably, checking that Sue was following me. Inside, I found a light switch and snapped it on. The neon tubes, flaring overhead, made us both blink.

The gallery was neat and tidy. Stairs led upwards towards the living quarters. I stepped forward and saw, in the typewriter by the photocopier so neatly placed, a sheet of paper still in the typewriter's roller carriage. Typed centrally, in capitals, were the words that stopped me. They said:

I'M SORRY TIM.

I stared at the words in total confusion. What in hell was this?

'I'm sorry, Tim?' Sue read it out loud, standing beside me. 'That's almost—Tim, that's almost like a suicide note!'

The sound of the generator throbbing outside the back door but inside the stable, made me shriek out loud and run, back through the kitchen to the scullery and out into the yard where the sound of that throbbing was now raucously hoarse and dominant in my ears.

The big black central double doors were locked with a padlock and hasp. I wrenched at the padlock in futile fury.

'Next door!' Sue was beside me, thinking, not attacking like me.

The next set of doors were locked as well, but not with a padlock and hasp; this time it was an old keyhole lock without a key. The doors were loose and rattled as I hammered at them. At the bottom I got a purchase by hooking my fingers under a rotted bit of plank near the ground and heaved forward. The door creaked and groaned but the lock tongue still held engaged. I got both hands under one door, braced my legs and heaved. Satisfying, splintering noises came from the centre joint. Sue put her arms around my waist and together we made one more massive heave, nearly falling over backwards as the lock snapped free and the door swung sharply open. Out in the yard I smelt the fumes and heard the engine running, phutting and popping from a badly rusted exhaust.

'Keep back!' I shouted at Sue and ran into the stable.

Walls separated each bay from each set of doors, but they didn't go up the full height of the building. I jumped, got a finger grip on the top of a dividing wall and swung myself up. Below me, as I poised on the narrow top edge of brick, I saw the light grey roof of a rusty Morris Minor 1000 in the centre bay. The car drummed happily as its engine vibrated. From the exhaust pipe at the back a piece of rubber hose ran round the car to the driver's side window. I took a deep breath, face averted, and dropped down beside the vehicle. It took me fifteen seconds to leap round to the driver's side, breath held, open the front door and remember that the ignition key on a Minor is in the centre of the dashboard somewhere. I switched off with a wrench that nearly snapped it. The engine stopped.

I found that I was hard up against Amanda Stanley's generous body in the driving seat. Her bleached blonde hair had been let down from its bandanna and lay around her face and shoulders like a false golden tide, spilling down the dark jumbled gown to where the odd ripe yellow banana peeped out to match it.

CHAPTER 17

'They're building a new hospital in Hastings,' Foster said without enthusiasm, looking morosely at the long green corridor and its clutter. 'Out on the ridge. Ultra-modern, it's going to be. Cost of millions.'

'Oh really?' I blew on a scrape I'd given my knuckles and thought yet again that it had been acquired either when I went over the dividing wall or, more likely, when I hooked my fingers under one of the outside doors to pull it open. Either way it wasn't a bad enough scrape to bring to the attention of anyone in the hospital building, where the usual congested passages with high frosted windows were lit against the grim November evening by livid tubes that made even Sue's healthy face look pallid, dark-eyed and anxious. Well: she was anxious. No, not a bad enough scrape to bring to the attention of anyone but stinging enough to keep nagging me about itself and what I'd been doing and how it had marked me for a period it would itself determine.

'Still—' Foster took the silence that followed my dull, uninterested reply to mean that I wasn't going to speak again and was absolutely right— 'I don't suppose that they'll get to the scene any quicker than these boys did after your call. Pretty good, really. And you giving her the kiss of life; rugger training has its uses even if it's not really designed to counteract the effects of drugs and carbon monoxide, I must say.'

One of the effects of carbon monoxide poisoning is to reduce the oxygen supply to the brain. Carbon monoxide, if you want to be technical, combines readily with the hæmoglobin of the blood and stops it carrying oxygen round the body. If enough oxygen doesn't get to the brain, the damage to the brain is irreversible. I knew all this from first aid lectures I'd been to and, I had no doubt, so did Foster.

My efforts in the yard outside the stable were probably quite futile but I had to make quite sure that Amanda kept breathing until the ambulance, summoned by Sue, arrived. We were doing what most visitors to hospitals do, which is to wait and hope while doctors carry out tests and consider things before they tell you very little.

'The good thing,' I said, feeling that some response was necessary although I didn't feel like it, 'is that there wasn't any exertion on her part. She must have been out cold, drugged I suppose, so she couldn't exert herself. Exertion uses up the oxygen bloody fast and then you're done for. Amanda was sitting still, hardly breathing but sitting still.'

He nodded hopefully. 'The better thing is that that bloody Minor's exhaust system was so full of holes that the fumes were farting out all over the place from under the car before they got down the pipe and into the interior. The whole building was infused, but the levels, fortunately, were low. Well, relatively low. Mind you, it's a wonder you weren't asphyxiated getting to the car.' He chewed on something imaginary in his mouth for a moment. 'That bloody car. Right under our noses in Hastings all the time.'

'It's not surprising that you didn't find it.' Sue was sympathetic. 'Locked away in that coach-house or stable or whatever that old block is. But it must have been driven down there on that same Saturday morning, after we'd seen it at the garage, and been put away very quickly.'

'So much for my clever theories about lock-up garages.' Foster did another chew on the imaginary obstacle in his mouth. 'So much for door to door work. We took her word, of course. My lads would be bound to. Known her for so long.' He scowled. 'It's always the obvious thing, isn't it? Your friend Roberts said that to me. It's what you want to believe that fools you.' He stared at Sue appraisingly, letting the frown dissipate. 'Bloody clever of you to see that about her painting being the same as Sedgwick's. I wonder if she guessed that you'd rumbled her during your last visit to the gallery?'

'She might have.' Sue sounded dubious. 'I think it was Tim talking about you and lock-up garages that prompted things to go off the rails.'

'Whatever it was—' I was still churning events around in my mind—'she didn't try to commit suicide, anyway. You don't fix yourself up in a car like that and then lock the doors from the outside. It was the most ham-handed attempt to fudge a murder to look like suicide that I've ever heard of. I mean, *I'm sorry Tim.* Bloody ridiculous.'

Foster stared at me strangely for a moment and then shook his head gently. 'I'm afraid I've been saving this one for you until things died down a bit. You didn't have to batter your way in from the outside, gallant though it was. There's a connecting door to the back of the gallery from inside the stable block. It was unlocked. It's on the opposite side of the house from the kitchen where you went in. You have to go out of the gallery at the back into a hallway where the stairs are. The connecting door to the stable is at the end of another old scullery or washroom off that hall. You couldn't have known, being in the hurry you were. Although the Morris is in the centre stable there's another door between the front stable and it, at the back beyond the bonnet of the car. You ripped your way into the third stable which only has access from outside, apart from going over the interconnecting wall. So it could have been a suicide attempt. I hope she'll be able to clarify that for us, though. When she comes round.'

Foster and Sue were looking at me intently all of a sudden. It made me feel alienated. I also felt like an imbecile. I got up abruptly and went along the passage to the men's washroom to rinse my knuckles. That just about put the lid on it. If ever there was a piece of symbolism for you, there it was: me battering my blundering way in from the outside into the wrong stable while all the time anyone in the know had an inside passage to slip along, to arrive quietly at their chosen destination. Me, putting the wrong gloss on everything. The whole affair was like a building, like the gallery, like a fortress intimately known to its defenders while the fools outside rode round trumpeting, trying to get in. Guessing and hurling themselves at stone walls. Futile. If I'd stopped to explore, to go to the other side of the gallery, at the back, I'd have found the connecting door to the old stables. But not me; I just blundered typically along the trodden path I knew, dealing with the territory I'd already seen, like a bull at a gate. All right, so I'd got Amanda Stanley out in the end, in my own blathering way, mainly thanks to Sue, but so what? Anyone who'd stopped to think could simply have walked into the stable. This whole business was like that; me charging around, up and down from London to Hastings like a yo-yo, turning up on site to find disasters, formulating theories that were half-baked, wagging my tail at blondes like a faithful old dog, egged on by a half-amused wife and boss like an old chaser being given a chance to gallop round a familiar course once again while the real runners were absent. It was pathetic; I was pathetic. Nobby and Foster were just like the rest, watching, amused, while I turned over some stones at the edge of a trail they were blazing, a trail they knew, had the map for, could predict the course of.

A trail they both knew? Was that why I was so angry?

I shook myself. It was pathetic. The theory about Knewstub was probably pathetic, too. *Proserpine* was most likely a painting from the period when a man called Treffry Dunn was Rossetti's assistant, not Knewstub. I was becoming like Rossetti myself, pursuing mediæval and romantic ideals while Nobby and Foster stuck to Truth to Nature. It was a bugger's muddle. I was sick of it.

I looked at myself in the washroom mirror. That face had grinned and moved and spoken knowingly to Amanda Stanley, telling her this and telling her that as she smiled and flattered me while Sue, all the time, had been looking at that view with St Clement's Church in it, assessing it and the other drawings. That face was not popular with me.

I splashed the face, dried it and my hands on a stained

roller towel and marched out of the washroom, slamming the bloody door behind me. In the green cluttered passage Sue and Foster were still waiting patiently. They looked up sharply as I stalked rapidly towards them.

'Right.' I directed myself to Sue. 'That's enough. We're going.'

'Tim?'

'Going. Off. Time to leave. Let's go.'

Her mouth opened in surprise. Foster frowned, slightly, puzzled.

'There's no point in hanging about here. We're not needed. Nothing we can do. Come on.'

'But—but don't you want to wait to find out how Amanda is?'

'What good will waiting do?' My voice sounded unusually harsh. 'There's nothing we can do. We are entirely superfluous. Not needed.'

'Tim?'

'Amanda's in good hands. We are completely unnecessary. And have been all along. A pair of supernumeraries. Come on.'

'Hey, take it easy.' Foster stood up. 'Hold on.'

I took Sue's arm, not very carefully. 'For God's sake! Come on!'

'Tim! Stop it! What is the matter with you?'

'I'm going. Back to London. Now.'

She put her hand on mine, the one holding her arm. 'You're upset. What's happened?'

'I'm sick of blundering round like a bloody horse in a bog. Out! I'm out! I'm off. Are you coming or not?'

'I'm coming.' She picked up her handbag. I saw her and Foster exchange glances. 'I'm coming. I would like to have heard whether she's going to be all right or not. I would have liked that.'

'We can phone. They won't tell us anything anyway. They never do. They won't know for a while. We're just extras. In the way. Dupes. They won't tell us anything more than he or Nobby would.' I gesticulated at Foster to emphasize my point. 'Come on.'

Foster was still standing. 'What's up? What's got into you?'

'I'll tell you if you like: I've learnt my lesson. You and Nobby have had a good laugh and now the joke's over. The professionals have got it all to themselves. Goodbye.'

He shook his head. I took Sue along the passage and out through some swing doors to where the car was parked on the freezing wet tarmac outside. I saw her in and slammed the door. I was stamping around the front of the car when I became aware that Foster was standing in the light of the hospital doorway and staring out at me, his face pale against his dark clothes.

'They've just said that she'll pull through,' he called. 'At least the tests are all encouraging. They hope there won't be any permanent damage. It's a good chance, apparently. I don't think you were such a supernumerary. She'd have been dead otherwise.'

I didn't reply to that.

'I'm going to be able to interview her later.' Foster sounded anxious. 'Don't you want to wait?'

I got in and slammed the Jaguar's door.

'Please,' Sue said as I started the engine. 'Don't kill us on the way back.'

I didn't reply to that, either. I was going to drive like hell. Women may get angry, women may inflict enormous, fatal damage, but for sheer red bloody murderous rage you need a man every time. Nothing helped: nothing. I had come to know what the roles were in that clever letter of Sedgwick's.

That was the problem; I could see it all too clearly.

I was the sheep.

Derek Sedgwick was the goat.

And I had a damned good idea, now, what the bloody soap was all about.

CHAPTER 18

'Laundering,' I said, as we got through the hall in Onslow Gardens and headed up the stairs. 'That's what this was all about. Laundering. Of money. Boringly enough, some of it was to do with drugs. Boringly enough, some of it was to do with what are known as third party commissions. That's what that Japanese was after, as Nobby hinted. Soap; laundering embarrassing money.'

We had driven back from Hastings in record time but it was now very late; into the early hours. I had not spoken much on the way back and felt guilty about it. Reaction had set in. Anti-climax. I felt drained. Sue was quiet, making me feel even more guilty. She had encouraged me in what she felt was in my own best interests and I had repudiated the whole thing. I had been fooled by a practically panto-mime blonde while she had kept her wits about her.

Sue had liked Amanda Stanley, liked her enough to look so closely at her work. I thought about the gallery, those strong paintings, and shivered. I didn't want to accept what those paintings and the bright New Orleans scenes meant. Not at all. Everything I had taken in, I had taken in falsely. What I had been was another sheep, one being led on— what was it?—like a lamb to the slaughter. I had been a decoy for another supposed flock of sheep: the Japanese. To impress them, to show how close, how far back our relationship went, Derek Sedgwick had written to me via our old College. The Japs would think that very important, would believe that such things really count. Mr Taganaki had, I was sure, seen my reply promising to visit. When he got to that cottage my reply was waiting and someone showed it to him, either Derek Sedgwick or Monica Haines. If anything could have accelerated the deal he was being pressured to close, my note would have.

Taganaki and his colleagues would have checked up on me, of course, they would be very thorough about things like that. They would have found that I did indeed manage an Art Fund even if Derek's advice that I was internationally famous was a blatant exaggeration. I could see him saying it, though, telling the Jap that he, Derek, had an inside track to the leading British art fund, to the very manager of it, someone who would snap up a Rossetti or two like a seal getting its fish at the zoo. The Japs would never have heard of me otherwise, despite Mr Okanura's pleasant flattery. I was the sheep in every direction. I had been set up to chase non-existent Pre-Raphaelites by what seemed to be a reference to Holman Hunt and Millais, a reference the Japs would understand and a reference that would keep me off the real scent. I had been set up to stimulate the Japs to clinch a deal. I had been set up by Nobby and Foster, I had no doubt of it, to chase strong muscular art hares across irrelevant fields while they watched what real quarry could be flushed out by my activities, what real quarry in international fraud and drug carriage they could capture and enhance their reputations with. They hadn't even rumbled the falsely-signed paintings, supposedly Sedgwick's, marketed by Jane Lardner and Doug Rostin. None of that. They probably weren't important to them. I hadn't been meant to get the Rossetti and I hadn't been meant to solve any police cases. I was just being used, as so often before, by everyone who needed a mug for their own ends.

I was still hopping mad.

The only thing that gave me any satisfaction was the near-death of Amanda Stanley, probably an attempted murder. I still believed that. It was only a satisfaction in that it showed that something had gone very wrong, not that I would have wished that sort of harm to Amanda. I could now imagine what panic-stricken conversations there must have been above that gallery. Her so-called suicide attempt was evidence of a major crisis. It was also something Foster and Nobby hadn't counted on. If there was any consolation to be had from all these events, my battering my way into the stable block was it. It was still symbolic, though, symbolic of my outsider status, my ridiculous role as a bit-part player feeling humiliated because he hadn't been given a star's position. In future I'd stay out of this. It was now up to Foster and Nobby to pull in Derek Sedgwick and finish off the job. They'd need me as a witness, that's all; I was the only person who'd seen that Morris Minor clearly at the garage, who could link it directly with the murder of the garage man. Not even Sue could do that; seated in the Jaguar that fatal Saturday morning, out of the cold, she hadn't even glanced at the Minor from the warm cockpit. Only I had done that. In a sense, despite all the other things that had happened to me, most of them second-hand, that was the key sighting of this affair. I had my ideas about it but they'd need verifying, later, when all this was over.

When all this was over.

'Do you know,' I said to Sue, putting my key into the lock of the flat's front door, 'when all this is over I think we should go for a holiday. I think we need to get some distance between us and the art world for a bit.'

'What a good idea.'

It wasn't Sue's voice. Her mouth hadn't moved. The voice came from above and behind me and it was masculine. I whipped round from the door to look up the stairs and found myself staring at the barrels of a 12-bore shotgun held by the American, Doug Rostin. His blond hair gleamed in the stairlight and he crouched, tense, behind the gun, holding it levelled at my chest.

It wasn't Rostin who had spoken, though.

Behind him, still on the half-stair, stood Derek Sedgwick. It was he who had spoken. Under his arm he held not two barrels of a gun but two rolls of canvas, quite thick, pressed against the bulky, ill-fitting sweater he wore. He had on not shorts this time, but long thin drain-pipe cord trousers that clutched tightly at his knobby knees. His thin face had a flushed, high-temperature look.

'Hello, Tim,' he said, his voice pitched slightly high. 'I'm glad you've shown up. The landing up there was getting cold.' He took one step down towards us while Rostin didn't move. 'You shouldn't look so surprised to see me. I've come to sell you a couple of paintings.' He brandished the two canvases. 'Whether you like them or not.'

CHAPTER 19

Nemesis was the goddess of retribution. In modern parlance the word has come to mean a downfall that satisfies retributive justice. I should have known, of course. I should have thought it out. Where else was Derek Sedgwick going to go when, trapped over Amanda Stanley's gallery, deprived of his Japanese source of capital for the skulduggery he had set up, he was plotting and planning feverishly to escape from his claustrophobic situation? All along we had assumed he was in London or, at a stretch, in Spain forming an alibi. Jane Lardner seemed to be his most obvious escape route. Yet he was not there; he was not in Spain; and Rostin had been making calls to Hastings. It was obvious, it was clear, but I had ignored it, not wanting to accept the implication about Amanda Stanley and the lies she had so easily passed off on me. The moment I saw that pale grey Morris shape in the dark stable I should have known. Perhaps I did; but by then Sedgwick must have gone, heading for London to meet up with Rostin and set up this horrific meeting.

Nemesis. My Nemesis.

Who else would his mind focus upon when, from above Amanda's gallery, he thought his way out? Who else was on the scene, following him, talking blandly in the gallery below, revealing his every thought and move? Who else was a market for nineteenth-century British paintings, easily accessible, easily available, prompted by Sedgwick's own letter like a gun dog chasing hares? Who else was vulnerable enough?

Yes, vulnerable enough.

My anger had dissipated now; I was weary and drained. I had brought what I had brought upon myself. It was going to need something now, some inner resource, to stimulate my normal response to this kind of situation. Sue and I sat opposite each other on each end of the big sofa. Doug Rostin sat at the breakfast table by the window, holding the shotgun pointed at us. The lights were low and all the curtains were drawn. Derek Sedgwick stood in front of us near the empty fireplace, where he had unrolled the two canvases.

'There we are,' he said, keeping his voice low. '*Proserpine*. And a half-finished oil sketch of the head of Fanny Corn-forth. A study for *Found*, of course, as you will both know. A theme it took thirty years for Rossetti to complete and of which there are eighteen known studies plus a replica by Treffry Dunn. You are going to buy both of them.'

'Oh, am I?'

'Yes. You are. The painting of *Proserpine* will cost you three-quarters of a million and the study for *Found* a mere fifty thousand. Eight hundred thousand pounds. A bargain, I'd say.'

'They're fakes.' Sue's voice was sharp, firm. I found it glorious that despite Rostin's horrible presence, she had such courage.

'My dear Mrs Simpson, we have not met before but I do advise you not to be hasty. What is a fake? What is reality?' Sedgwick turned to me. 'I loved your trail after Knewstub, Tim. It was characteristic of you. Brilliant. The Japs swallowed it hook, line and sinker too, when I put it to them, but you got there alone. Amanda liked it too, of course, being a Manchester girl. Here I had a receipt for two paintings bought in a junk shop in Hastings. Pre-Raphaelite School. And there I have the very things. Or have I? It does not matter. What is reality? See how you, with all your expertise, were prepared to believe that a real Rossetti could fetch up among the flotsam of Hastings. Who else would not believe such a thing? Who, indeed, would not *want* to believe such a thing?' His voice rose slightly. 'There I was, rotting in that cottage on the bloody cliff edge. I knew all the history of art in Hastings from Willie the Conk to Letitia Yhap, so bloody well I could've screamed. Nothing else to do but starve and rot and read in the Public Library, read every damned thing with any reference to Hastings from Whistler to Mick Rooney. Banting and Burra getting pissed at the Nelson. No good, any of it. No use. Except the Knewstub story.'

A dreadful fear crept up my spine. 'The junk shop. Was it run by a Mrs Gallagher?'

'Clever Dick! Clever Tim! How did you know? She thought she was really on to something. She died, you know, of a heart attack.'

'After you'd got your receipt?'

'How did you guess?'

The fear had become a chill. There are a number of ways that a heart attack can be induced. Drugs are the most common.

'And then,' Sue's voice was still clear, 'whatever those Pre-Raphaelite School pieces were—an oil and a sketch, presumably—they became those fakes there?'

He scowled. He seemed taller than I remembered him, even scraggier, just as thin, but somehow more tattered. The bulky sweater had been pulled on over a wool shirt that had seen better days and the drainpipe cords were scuffed and stained. He had not shaved, I guessed, for about two days and his face was still flushed in a blotchy way that told of blood pressure and fatigue or nerves. The eyes were penetrating though, because dark rings round them emphasized their depth within the sockets. There was no strength about his body, no substance, but a kind of wire-strung tension that made his joints, his movements, jerky and slightly out of control. Rostin sat impassive, holding the shotgun, watching us all carefully.

'Be careful about the word fakes.' Sedgwick's voice rose very slightly. 'That oil sketch may well be by Treffry Dunn. I bought it a while ago and it has plenty of age. It could well be from Rossetti's studio.'

'What about her?' Sue pointed at *Proserpine*. Janey Morris's unmistakable features pouted sullenly above a split pomegranate. I didn't know who painted the copy but it was good, good enough to pass immediate viewing and possibly even quite old. The sort of canvas that followers of Rossetti might have painted not too long after his death in 1882 or, I supposed, almost any time up to about sixty years ago. No wonder old Mrs Gallagher had become excited, if this was one of her 'Pre-Raphelite School' paintings.

Sedgwick smiled at Sue's question and flourished a wave of the arm at the sultry portrait. 'I'm sure Tim's bank will enjoy owning her.'

'No chance.' My voice was a growl.

The smile vanished. 'Perhaps you won't enjoy her. But own her you will.'

'Why?'

'One of the great things about banks is that they have money. Cash. Since I've been deprived of my rightful sale to that bloody Japanese I'm sure it's only fitting that you step into the breach. You are the ideal man, Tim. Tomorrow morning when the Bank opens you will withdraw eight hundred thousand pounds in cash. You will give it to me and I will give you these two pictures. No less honest than that.'

'You must be crazy.'

His flush deepened. 'Don't you speak to me like that! You fat cats with a bank! Just like Mr Taganaki.'

'You'd never have got away with that. The Japs would never have paid up without checking.'

'Ah, but that's where you're wrong, Mr Clever Tim! Bloody wrong! Mr Taganaki was a greedy bastard. He was given a budget of one and a half million pounds to spend. Petty cash for the Tamanoshaganaki Corporation. What is art to people like that? He could buy my paintings for eight hundred thousand pounds and put seven hundred thousand away in Switzerland. Were you clever enough to think of that?'

I nodded slowly. 'I thought so. I didn't know the exact figures but I guessed that was it. You'd give him an invoice for one and a half million. He'd pay you and you'd then send seven hundred thousand to his private account somewhere. He goes back to Japan with a famous Rossetti of *Proserpine*, a full sketch of Fanny Cornforth for *Found*, and a provenance you've built for him involving Walter John Knewstub and his son Jack and Hastings. Who would not want to believe it, as you say? Deception in art is all in the buyer's mind.'

Sedgwick smiled again. 'I can see that banking and art have sharpened your wits, Tim. That was something like it. Something like it.'

'And you had a sale of one and a half million with only eight hundred thousand coming to you. That meant that you could launder seven hundred thousand pounds' worth of drug money that your friend Rostin there is anxious to legitimize.'

There was a silence. Rostin shifted uncomfortably and cleared his throat, but the shotgun did not waver. His presence, so quiet and observant, made an icy contrast to the feverish-looking Sedgwick. They were a difficult double act, complementing each other in the execution of actions that were unthinkable, that could not be contemplated. Yet Rostin looked as though he might just have stepped off a golf course in Georgia: suntanned, easy-going yet controlled, casual yet muscular. Sedgwick looked like a derelict from one of the cardboard-carton dormitories under a Thames bridge. His smile was as brittle as a plastic umbrella rib.

'Soap, Derek,' I said. 'That was the soap part. Your little *double entendre* about sheep, goats and soap. Who was going to care if seven hundred thousand disappeared briefly and then reappeared again? You would have had a bill of sale for one and a half million and exactly one and a half million in the bank. Eight hundred thousand from the Jap and seven hundred thousand from your pal Doug here. Not a bad split for the two of you. Legitimately deposited. The fact that the painting is a fake and the seven hundred grand comes from some filthy trade is neither here nor there. You could then arrange to pay as little tax as possible on this money. I don't suppose the sale would be made anywhere where you'd pay much tax anyway.'

Sedgwick's flush had faded. His thin scraggy face peered down at me, staring directly at me. Rostin, after his throat noises, was dead quiet again.

'That deals with the soap. You were the goat. Not a sacrificial goat. A goat with women. You always were. Monica Haines and Jane Lardner and Amanda Stanley. All yours. At some time or another, possibly even concurrently. All short of money. Haines for her drugs and the other two for their art galleries. All willing to help. To fool the sheep; the Japs and me. Amazing.'

'Fantastic.' His voice was incredulous. 'Absolutely fantastic. The reference was nothing like that. It was just the Pre-Raphaelites. You've built your own mad version of it. Mad. There was no *double entendre*.'

'Let's just say that it's an interpretation I like. One I've built for myself. I think maybe it was subconscious on your part, though. Everything went well about it except the goat part.'

'The goat part? What rubbish is this?'

'Sure. The goat part.' I gave Sue a quick smile. She was sitting straight up, legs not crossed, looking straight at me. She'd been in some unpleasant situations with me before but somehow this had not yet got to the point of terror. I couldn't see Sedgwick going in for shotgun killings, the bloody blast of a 12-bore. I assumed the gun must have come from Lark's Farm Cottages or a similarly rural source and that did make me a bit nervous because rural shotguns can be unreliable. I had to keep talking. 'The goat part? Monica Haines first. Amanda Stanley second. Where's the elegant Jane Lardner, by the way? In the getaway car?'

There was no answer. Sedgwick glanced quickly at Rostin, who tightened his grip on the gun. I had a sudden flash of insight that told me maybe they'd killed her too, or planned to, once they'd got the money. I thought that Monica Haines had probably double-crossed Sedgwick over the Jap and that Amanda Stanley, getting cold feet, had tried to back out of things, but I didn't suppose that Sedgwick would volunteer that information. So far, he probably didn't know that Amanda had survived and could give us her version in due course. He was staring at me, white of face.

'Talking of getaway cars,' I said, suddenly feeling more confident, 'I must say it was bad luck when that old josser Bengate impounded your car when you were on the way to the cottage with the paintings. I suppose you still owed him money despite Amanda's efforts at painting on your behalf? And don't tell me you sold well in New Orleans. You never sold at all. Nor did poor Amanda's work with your signature on it. That was a laundering operation, too.' I gestured at Rostin. 'For him. I expect you met him through Monica Haines, who took drugs. What was the business? Crack? Cocaine? The good thing was that Rostin there had the Jap connection for you. You'd never have been credible yourself. Did Taganaki take drugs too?'

'You talk too much.' Rostin's voice, suddenly sounding, was still low, Southern, imbued with a stylish menace. 'Much too much. We don't want to hear any more from you. Nothing. You just shut up, and let me do the talking.'

There was an authority about the quiet Southern accent that chilled the room. Sedgwick's flushed presence had none of the calm impression of control that Rostin emanated. I had the feeling that Rostin was almost an observer of what was happening rather than part of it, but his grasp of the shotgun was real enough and his unbudging posture showed no sign of nerves. He leant forward. 'In the morning, first thing, you are going to your bank with Derek there and you're going to draw out that money. First thing. Because if Derek doesn't phone me in here by ten a.m. tomorrow saying he's got the eight hundred thousand in cash then your lady there is going to have a very unpleasant experience. Understand me? Understand me real good?'

'But that's impossible! I can't just draw out that much!'

'You'll find a way. You call an emergency, Mr Banker, because you've got one. Unless you hand that money over to Derek things are going to get real nasty for Mrs Simpson.'

'We're a merchant bank not a clearance house. We're not full of cash.'

Rostin grinned. It was a grin meant to intimidate, a grin smeared over his deliberate ignoring of what I said. He continued almost as if I hadn't spoken. 'If Derek phones in saying OK, then I'll just walk out of here and leave your lady tied up for you to come and release. You'll see me tie her up before you leave. The longer I wait after ten o'clock the more I might just take advantage. And if there's any clever tricks—dye on the notes, or if you grab Derek— then—' he patted the barrels of the 12-bore—'I won't hesitate to use this. Get me? Understand me? I got a lot riding on this deal. Any hitch, and I'll get nasty.'

'For God's sake!' I turned to Derek Sedgwick. 'You can't—you can't do this! It's crazy!'

His reply was to smile. The blotchy patches to his face had returned, as though he had absorbed what I'd said about his schemes and recovered from it. It was like looking at a copy of the Derek Sedgwick I'd known at College, a Tussaud version not in waxwork but some other, more realistic material that was like human flesh but wasn't. The coffee-drinking, recreational wastrel and the hopeless artist had disappeared into the desperate skeleton of the criminal in front of me, yet it was hard to believe that this really was a criminal, that this was another human being of normal inclinations only slightly altered by some external source to become a jerky, unprincipled victim of his own fantasies.

He didn't reply. He just smiled that smile across the mottled look of his face. For the first time I became really frightened. Beside him, spread open, the lush landscape of Proserpine's pouting red lips and tumbled dark hair was deathly sinister. Derek Sedgwick was over the top; he had gone beyond the point of no return. I flashed a quick glance at Doug Rostin, impassive and blond behind the shotgun;

I had assumed him to be the *éminence grise* behind everything that had happened but now I was not so sure. Sedgwick was out of control. Rostin might not be able to influence things as much as I had assumed. For all that he was clearly the source and organizer of the drugs side of things, presumably with influence and professional power, he might not have such sway over the now unpredictable being that Sedgwick had beome.

Perhaps he intended to dispose of Sedgwick when all this was done. As the thought hit me I addressed myself to him, turning to look directly at him.

'You tie up my wife at your peril.'

A surprised look stiffened his face. 'What?'

'I said you tie up my wife at your peril. If you so much as touch her I'll kill you.'

Rostin's face changed to a sneer. 'Brave boy! I don't think you quite appreciate the situation here, Simpson.' He gestured with the shotgun, making me flinch.

'Tim.' Sue's voice was warning.

I leant towards him. 'Don't be too clever, Doug. That shotgun looks very rural to me. I bet Derek here snitched it from Lark's Farm. One good pull on the trigger and it'll probably blow up in your face.'

I shot a glance at Sedgwick. His face told me that my guess about the source of the gun was probably true. Rostin, however, showed no timidity, and with a sinking feeling I guessed that someone as cool as him would have checked the gun out carefully.

'I might just try it.' He smiled the same unemotional smile he had smeared over his face before. 'How about that? Should I?'

'You'd lose your money if you did. You can't pull that trigger and get me to go to the bank.

For the first time, his face became angry. 'I might just blow your leg off. Then your lady can go to the bank to make sure you don't bleed to death.'

'And have every policeman in London plus the SAS come

and get you, Rostin? No, that won't work. Your only hope is to make sure I stay in one piece until morning. That way you just might get your money. But I warn you: tie up Sue or touch her and I'll follow you to bloody New Orleans or wherever you hide and I'll hammer you flat. I promise you.'

He leered at me. 'Tough talk. I've heard talk like that from too many like you. And dealt with them.'

'Like old Bengate at the garage? Your partner there made a real mess of things, didn't he? Got his car impounded, found the Jap and Monica in bed, lost his mind, blew them up and sent for you. Unreliable, isn't he?'

'Shut up! Just shut up! I'm sick of listening to you!' Rostin got to his feet and jabbed the shotgun in my direction. 'Any more and I'll finish it! Hear me? Finish it!'

Sedgwick stared at him. Mingled fear and agreement chased across his face. I sat quite still and glared at Sue. She was frozen rigid, still sitting upright in the other corner of the sofa. Her white face made her eyes look huge. For a moment Rostin poised in front of us, the gun held tight into his side. Then he relaxed a little and shook his head.

'No more talk,' he said. He gestured at Sue. 'No more talk. You, lady, go over to that kitchenette and make coffee. Strong coffee. No funny tricks. We all have to keep nice and wide awake until morning. All of us. Until we get that money.'

CHAPTER 20

You read sometimes, in the papers, about some luckless bank manager who, with his family, is impounded all night by robbers until he can open the vaults in the morning. It had never occurred to me that, even though I work in what is technically a bank, such a thing could happen to me. The Art Fund and my departmental duties in overseas investment were not things that I had ever thought of as capable of generating a kidnap night. But it was happening: it was unreal, impossible to believe. It was happening.

Even the phone never rang. I half-expected Foster to call me from Hastings to tell me what Amanda Stanley might have said, but there was nothing. I supposed that in view of my mood when we'd left the hospital car park he decided not to disturb me until morning. Yet surely the crisis in Hastings must be precipitating action of some sort?

After a while Sue and I sat closer on the settee and she put her head on my shoulder. She didn't sleep, at least I don't think she did, but she closed her eyes. Outside, there were the noises of a London residential street, mainly cars, for a while, but they died down before dawn and it became quiet. Sedgwick sat in an armchair but Rostin stayed at the table on which he had placed the shotgun, and kept himself upright. His bronzed face stared almost unwinking into the room. It all seemed ridiculous, absurd, the sort of thing that no one could get away with, but did. They must surely have realized that no one can draw eight hundred thousand pounds from a bank, any bank, on his own say-so, just like that, without clearance. They must surely have realized I would have to tell someone at the Bank, like Jeremy, why I really needed the money. I could not even understand why I should be left with the painting of Proserpine and the sketch, if I was going to be, but perhaps I wasn't. This was a straight ransom demand in reality, but perhaps in Derek Sedgwick's warped sense of trade it was a form of justice, of retribution, that I should be left with the objects he had so nearly sold to the luckless Mr Taganaki while he took the money.

From time to time I looked at him surreptitiously. He had killed Monica Haines and Taganaki. I thought he had probably tried to kill Amanda Stanley. I wondered what he had done with or intended to do to Jane Lardner. In my reluctant subconscious I guessed he had no intention that I should survive, either. And that meant Sue was intended to go as well. If Rostin was to stay in the flat with the shotgun, then how could Derek Sedgwick kill me? He certainly wasn't strong enough, physically. If he had no gun, then how would it happen? How had he killed before?

Dynamite?

I flashed another glance at him. He didn't seem to have enough about him to be carrying dynamite. He could have secreted it somewhere downstairs, though, waiting until— until what?

Until I got in the car?

It became fixed in my mind, then, that if he said we were to go to the Bank in my car, that would be it. He'd make me bring the money to the car, drive somewhere where he could safely get out and disappear, and tell me to drive off. And bingo! At some point afterwards up I would go, car and all. He knew how to set a charge. He knew how to set a timed charge, as they do in quarries. It was him, that dark night, scrambling down that tumbled cliff face pushing just enough into a crevice just far down enough. Of course! That would be it; he would allay my fears by appearing to go to the Bank unarmed, so that I would be free to return to Sue without worry. And under the car would be the charge, waiting, just waiting for the timer to click and complete the circuit.

If he said we would go to the Bank in my car, then that would be the telling decision. But he'd have to go down alone first, to put his charge in place. I chanced another glance at him; he was staring straight at me, pale-faced, as though reading my thoughts. For a moment I thought he was going to speak, but his thin countenance stared straight at me, unmoving.

He must have arrived unexpected at that cottage. On foot, of course, so there was no sound of the Morris's perforated exhaust pipe roaring and popping as there usually would have been. Did he have the canvases with him or had he had to leave them in the car, in its boot, when old Bengate refused him petrol and retained the car against his return with some cash?

Of course; he'd gone on to the cottage to get some cash from Monica or the Jap. Derek Sedgwick didn't own a credit card. Monica would have set it all up, most probably, not Sedgwick. Foster had said that she was the key. So had Nobby. She would have introduced Derek Sedgwick to Rostin, her supplier. Hence to the Jap. She would have seen herself as the prime mover, not a female appendage. Derek was useful, his deal with the Rossetti would stake out a really good working capital for them. Them? Perhaps Monica Haines hand't thought in terms of them. Perhaps Derek Sedgwick hadn't been part of her future plans.

He must have phoned Rostin, after the collapse of the cottages, to come and get him. All the way from London. And whether the canvases were in the car or not, he needed an alibi that exonerated him from being anywhere near Hastings, just in case. What a cock-up. The old man at the garage had probably made difficulties so Rostin clouted him. End of old Bengate. Then quick, hide the Morris at Amanda's while Rostin drove his hire car—or would it have been Jane Lardner's car?—back to London.

What a panic it must have been. Foster was right. No Master Plan, no concept; just a cock-up.

Or was this just the exhaustion of the early hours getting on my mind, making me think too much, too dangerously? It was getting light; past six o'clock. The Bank didn't open until nine. There was no point in going early. The streets were starting to move again, traffic was trundling down the Old Brompton Road in the distance. Someone got into a parked car across the gardens and drove off; the milk-float delivering our milk whined its electric way round from the far edge of the gardens and clattered its bottles.

The milk-float? Now? Ernie?

The milkman stopped next door. We heard him clatter a crate off the float and his boots slapped smartly up the stairs to the next house's front door. Derek Sedgwick stirred himself, looked at Rostin, turned back to me.

'We'll go to the Bank in your car,' he said. 'I don't want to be seen on public transport and you might give me the slip and try something funny. Just remember: she'll be all right as long as we get the money.'

Our milkman never stepped smartly. Not old Ernie.

'I can't park at the Bank,' I said. 'The traffic's terrible. It would be much better by Tube.'

'We'll take your car!' Sedgwick's voice rose neurotically. His sleepless reddened eyes glared at me. 'I'll wait outside in it. You'll deliver the money to me in the car, then you'll drive to a call-box I'll describe to you. If it's all OK, Doug will leave Sue here safe and sound. You can drive back straight away. No other arrangements. That's it.'

The milk-float wheezed into action from next door and pulled up under our windows. It suddenly hit me that this whole affair was going to begin and end with the milk.

'We need more milk,' I said. 'All the coffee has used up our pint. I'll—'

'Stay where you are!' Sedgwick's voice was still edgy. His face changed a little. 'Where's your car? That Jaguar of yours?'

'Across the gardens. On the other side. It's too early to leave yet. I need some coffee. With milk. I can't stand black coffee.'

Sue's hand, close to mine, took hold of it tightly. She knows I always drink tea for breakfast.

'Stay where you are.' Sedgwick nodded at Rostin. 'I'll go down and get a pint. You stay here.'

Rostin shook his head in amazement. 'They still deliver milk door to door here?'

'Yes. I'll go.'

That's it, I thought, that's when Sedgwick goes down and sticks the charge under my car. I stared at him as he shook himself and held a hand out to me.

'Come on,' he said. 'Give us the money for a pint.'

'We pay weekly. We have an account.'

'An account!' He sneered. 'Very clever. He won't know me, will he? So give us the money!'

'Just tell him it's for Mr Simpson. That's all you need to do.'

'I will.' He sneered again and straightened his bulky pullover. I could hear the milkman putting pints down on the front doorstep.

'Wait!' Rostin said suddenly, stopping Sedgwick where he was. 'I'm sick of sitting at this goddamn table. Here, you sit behind the gun and watch them. I'll stretch my legs and check on things. I have to see this milkman. Just in case.'

Sedgwick frowned. I saw his eyes flicker as he pondered this move. Could it be, I wondered, that Rostin planted the charges all along?

'Don't worry,' Rostin said to Sedgwick, almost in a consoling voice. 'You'll get plenty of exercise very soon.'

Sedgwick nodded and took over behind the shotgun. Rostin stepped across the living-room, through the entrance hall and went out of the flat's front door, leaving it open. I saw his blond hair disappear down the staircase well towards the lobby of the house.

'Don't move.' Sedgwick's voice was low but edgy, almost hoarse. He held the shotgun steady, its weight on the table, pointing in our direction. 'Once we've had some coffee we can start to get you on your way.'

'It's too early.'

'You'll do as I say! You have too big ideas about yourself, Mr Tim Simpson!'

His sleepless face focused itself jumpily on mine. It was the first time I had been alone with him since the whole business began and, despite Sue's intense grip, Rostin's brief absence gave me the chance to ask what had been on my mind since Nobby Roberts had been here, in this flat, the morning after we returned from our visit to Hastings.

'What was she going to do, Derek? Scarper with all your money and the Japanese?'

His mouth pulled down at the corners. One hand grasped the barrels of the shotgun, whitening at the knuckles.

'Must have been a shock. Standing unheard in the hallway of the cottage, in the dark, while they went at it upstairs and planned to cut you out.'

Downstairs I heard Doug Rostin open the front door and a whistle of winter street noise breezed faintly up the staircase. There was a voice, deep and masculine; Rostin said something in reply, probably giving my name.

'You were to be the mug in all this, weren't you, Derek?'

'Mug! Some bloody mug!' His voice thickened. 'I made the conniving bitch heave in ecstasy at the crunch!'

A milk bottle smashed on to the stone steps downstairs like the impact of an explosive charge.

Our heads shot up. There was a dull thud and a mumbled noise like a stifled voice. Sue's hand crushed over mine like a sash cramp.

Sedgwick came out from behind his table, shotgun at the ready. He brought its muzzles so close to my face that I could almost feel the press of cold metal circles against my cheek.

'Don't move,' he whispered. 'One move and you're gone.' His head cocked backwards. There was no further sound from the hall. 'Doug?' He called the name softly, over his shoulder.

There was no reply.

Sedgwick brought up a finger from the side of the shotgun.

'You sit there,' he whispered. 'You sit there. Just flinch and I'll pull the trigger. Just flinch.'

He backed towards the front door, holding the shotgun trained on us. Behind him, through the open door, I saw a milkman's hat come slowly up from the staircase well. Sue was going to cripple my hand for life; she could see the hat too.

Sedgwick got to the doorway, still facing us, going backwards. He half-turned to look out on to the stairway, not really seeing fully. 'Doug?' His voice was louder this time.

Behind him the head and shoulders of the milkman were now visible but he wasn't coming up the stairs the way any normal person would, forwards, his head down. He was coming up sideways, his back to the wall, his head up, trying to get a full view of our front door. He certainly wasn't Ernie, either; he was youngish and dark and fit-looking, with a clean-shaven face. I knew instinctively that he'd be one of Nobby Roberts's men. Suddenly he shouted, 'Police! Armed police! Freeze!'

Sedgwick turned a little further and, over his shoulder, saw the milkman. He swung sharply, bringing the shotgun with him, traversing the barrels in an arc, and I realized that the gun was below the line of the milkman's sight as Sedgwick crouched slightly with his knees to come into a firing position. I gave a shout of warning and prised Sue's hand off mine as I bounded off the sofa in an upward leap.

The shout and the movement distracted Sedgwick. He stopped in half-arc. His eyes, coming back round to meet mine, refocused and narrowed in hatred. The shotgun barrels traversed back again, swinging round quickly in an unmistakable pre-firing movement that could have only one intention. Sue screamed to me.

The sharp report of a police .38 revolver, loud and efficient, preceded the convulsive jerk of Sedgwick's body in the doorway. The muzzle of the shotgun's double barrels caught the door upright at his involuntary backward movement. The blast of the one barrel he fired before he died, going off outside into the stairway wall, blew little pieces of white plaster out into a cloud that pattered down slowly, like imitation snow, on to the grimy cords and bundled sweater of the thin, collapsed carcase on the doorstep.

CHAPTER 21

Nobby Roberts drank his fourth coffee of the morning and avoided my eye. The flat was more or less back to normal; more or less, that is, if you discount what the forensic men had done and the blanket over the patch at the front door where Derek Sedgwick had died and various things like that. Quite the normal domestic English scene, give or take a violent death and Inspector Foster sitting on the other side of the table drinking his third cup of coffee and eyeing the brandy I'd given myself and Sue but refusing it, reluctantly, on the grounds that he was still on duty despite having been up all night, but then hadn't we all? Been up all night, I mean.

'He listened to Monica Haines and the Jap in the bedroom,' Foster said. 'They were going to cut him out all right. She had it all planned. They were both to be signatories to the account and she regarded it as her deal. She'd brought Rostin and Taganaki into Sedgwick's orbit. To her he was just a rotten artist who'd turned up two passable possible Rossettis and had the background to make up a convincing provenance. She even fixed up the flow of Amanda Stanley's sub-contract work for Derek Sedgwick with Rostin. The money that came from New Orleans supposedly for those bright paintings was used to finance Monica Haines's dealings after they'd paid Amanda Stanley a fixed price per painting. Rostin wanted a way to transfer running costs to the UK.'

'Amanda Stanley told you all this?'

'At about two o'clock this morning, when they let me in to see her.' Foster gave me a reproachful glance. 'According to her version, Sedgwick appeared in a panic that Saturday morning saying the cottage had collapsed over the cliff with Haines and the Jap in it and that his car was impounded up at Bengate's. She drove him up to the garage, giving him money to pay for the car. She didn't realize, when he came out and drove the Minor away, that he'd clobbered old Bengate in a fit of rage.' Foster looked at me. 'It wasn't Rostin. He didn't come down from London to pick Sedgwick up. His role in this is either very unclear or else very cleverly played. Sedgwick didn't seem to think that Rostin was involved in the double-cross at all, yet Rostin was a contact of Monica Haines's originally. I think that Sedgwick trusted Rostin because they'd set up exhibitions in New Orleans together and that sort of thing. It does seem as though Haines was aiming to pull off a big one together with the Jap entirely for her own benefit. Sedgwick told Amanda Stanley—after she'd put his car away and hidden him for a day or so— what really happened because he knew she'd find out that the cottage collapse wasn't prompted by natural causes.' He sighed heavily. 'My men would have told her.'

'So Sedgwick told Amanda what had happened?'

'Oh yes. He'd learnt how to set charges from his quarry pal in Navarra. While doing it he kept three of them for himself somehow. They were in an outhouse at the cottage. We found one downstairs under your hall table.' Foster gave me a long stare before flashing a quick glance at Nobby. 'He promised Amanda Stanley a large slice of the future cake, of course.'

'So then she tried to commit suicide? Five days later?' I made it sound a bit more sarcastic than I intended, but I was still feeling a bit distraught.

'She doesn't remember anything about that. Nothing. When Sedgwick made his move I think he dealt with her. Drugged coffee. He probably typed that note.'

But for five days, I thought, Amanda Stanley played Sedgwick's game along with him, knowing what he'd done. How did he do it? He must have told Amanda how he'd stood inside the cottage, hearing every word and gasp of Monica Haines and Taganaki together upstairs, how in fury he had taken the charge he'd obtained from the quarryman in Navarra and clambered down the cliff to place it. How he must have watched as it exploded, muffled by the howling wind off the Channel, the whole awesome spectacle of a building with people in it disintegrating into splinters and rubble. And she hadn't cared enough to do anything but hide him in return for a slice of the cake and God knew what else.

'You knew, didn't you?' I said to Nobby Roberts. 'Or at least you guessed. You would never have sent me back down to Hastings to see Jerry Foster here and Amanda Stanley otherwise. Never. You had a pretty strong idea that Amanda Stanley was an accessory of some sort. To you, at your distance, it was a high probability. The local police were too close to her, knew her too well and liked her, but you calculated that she had a relationship of some kind with Sedgwick, not quite clear whether just commercial or otherwise, but something. You and Foster here couldn't prowl around all the time or keep visiting her, so you sent me. Us, I should say, Sue and me. And it worked. Sedgwick was flushed out. It made him act. I was your gun dog or, more likely, your beater.'

I glared at him but he was still avoiding my eye. I suppose what was really getting to me, making my voice angry, was not so much Nobby's deception at that lunch we'd had together—after all, I'd given him enough cause, with my baited remarks, to teach me a lesson—but Amanda Stanley's. Whatever deal Sedgwick intended to substitute for the Japanese once that was lost did, in the end, most likely involve extracting money from me by foul means. She must have had a good idea that that would be necessary and yet she had playacted her part impeccably. The deception had been excellent until I'd brought Sue on to the scene. She knew that those paintings wouldn't fool Sue, even if there had been any chance of fooling the Art Fund. I reached over and gave Sue's hand a gentle squeeze with my crushed one, the one she'd held so tightly. The irony was that, in the end, we'd saved Amanda's life.

'If it's any consolation—' Foster might have been reading my thoughts— 'it was because Amanda Stanley was having very powerful doubts and second thoughts that Sedgwick must have tried to get rid of her. She told him that he'd never pass off that Rossetti as genuine on your Fund, so he started to think of a more drastic scheme. After you'd brought your wife to meet her she told him he'd have to think of something else. That's the last major thing she remembers. It doesn't diminish her responsibility as an accessory to murder but I think it's true.' He paused and cleared his throat. 'I don't think we might have acted so quickly to cover your flat here and set up the milk entry scheme without her testimony. When we picked up the Lardner woman in the early hours of this morning it was clear that she didn't have such misgivings. She was packed, waiting for a phone call to head for the airport, in my view. She claimed total ignorance, of course, and will go on doing so. It will be hard to pin anything really concrete on her even though I believe she was a willing accessory to both Rostin and Sedgwick in the Japanese scheme and knew everything that was going on. She must have been livid when Sedgwick blew it. He literally blew it. He didn't even have the sense to keep his cool and outwit that Monica Haines woman. I think there was a massive dose of jealousy in that reaction of his, quite apart from the money.'

Jealousy, I thought, and alienation. A man living alone on top of that booming cliff in dire financial straits, staring at the waves while money sloshed around elsewhere, a man with a college education gone to ruins, a man doing nothing that anybody wanted and doing it badly. No wonder he lost contact with reality.

I thought of Jane Lardner, cool and bony, together with the carefully-controlled Rostin at the Vergam Gallery in Hammersmith. What sense of preservation kept them distanced like that while the other four people in the drama fractured themselves in the attempt? What had made Rostin instinctively hand over the shotgun to Sedgwick at the

moment that fatal danger threatened their enterprise?
Rostin, now in custody, would go to jail for some years on
our account and his role as accessory, if it could be proved,
but probably not for too long. Rostin and Jane Lardner
were the controllers, the manipulators who would never be
found on a howling cliff top in winter or actually putting
paint on to canvas themselves. I hated them much more
than the demented Sedgwick, victim of his own failures, or
Amanda Stanley, losing and trying, trying and losing. The
obstinacy of an old garage man, the mechanical condition
of an old car: on such things do the fate of people hinge.

'Well,' Sue said, giving Nobby a careful look, 'I'm pleased
to think that you made adequate preparations for us to be
protected, in view of all your plans. At first I didn't think
we'd be in any real danger, but then Derek Sedgwick turned
out to be not mentally stable. That was the terrifying part.
And, of course, quite a lot of things happened that weren't
really under control?'

She then put on an expression, still holding her gaze on
him, that combined the accumulated disapprobation of a
century of nanny-schoolmistresses with the righteous moral
censure of the Elders of a remote Scottish Wesleyan Chapel.
He wilted visibly.

'Look,' he mumbled, still avoiding a direct look, 'there
was nothing I could do to stop you short of arresting you
and I was a direct consultant to the Hastings force with a
duty to perform. I must admit that I didn't expect things
to turn out quite as they did in all directions. This is the
first time I've come across murder by house demolition on
the clifftops and I should have realized that anyone capable
of that is capable of anything. It was so hard to take
Sedgwick seriously—I thought Rostin, in London, would
be the focus of the really dangerous action even though
the information from Hastings and Spain all pointed at
Sedgwick.' He made a dismissive gesture. 'I'd known him
vaguely at College, you see, like Tim, and I always thought
of him as totally ineffective.' He focused on me at last. 'You

must admit you scoffed at the idea of Sedgwick's guilt, too, Tim.'

'True, I did.'

'Anyway—' he got up heavily—'I must be going. All the paperwork has to be seen to.' He waved down Foster, who had half-risen. 'Don't hurry. I'll see you back at the station. The squad has all been stood down.' He paused, looked at me, and turned to go.

'Nobby?' My question stopped him.

'What?'

'Next time we meet the lunch is on you.'

'Oh.' He flushed a little, then nodded cautiously. 'Oh, er, all right.' A sheepish grin came to his face before he brightened a little and looked at Sue. 'I completely forgot. Gillian asked me to ask you to lunch on Sunday. That was yesterday. What with one thing and another I, um, I forgot. Would you—that is—if you'd rather—'

'Of course we will.' Sue got up and kissed him on the cheek. 'We'd love to. It's all right, you know, Nobby.'

'Oh. Good.' He cleared his throat, patted her, nodded to me and Foster and walked to the door. Once there, alone, he turned back to look at me again. I shook my head sadly.

'What is it?' he demanded defensively. 'What are you shaking your head for now?'

'You,' I said, 'have forgotten your walking stick. Completely.'

I pointed at it, hanging on the chair opposite. And that was when we all started to laugh, so much that Foster, reviving, asked for a brandy after all, a large one, and Nobby came back and sat down again and had an even larger one himself.

CHAPTER 22

'They've reneged!' Jeremy White's eyes were rolling wildly. 'Absolutely reneged!' He waved the letter at me. 'It's a disgrace! A man's word is supposed to be his bond!'

'Jeremy,' I said patiently, 'you haven't even got a Rossetti to sell to them. So what are you making such a fuss for?'

'That doesn't matter! It's the principle of the thing! They offered to buy a Rossetti from us. It was a definite offer. Now that man Okanura says that due to market circumstances and the number of fake Impressionists about—as though that had anything to do with it—and the death of Mr Taganaki in embarrassing circumstances, his board has withdrawn its decision. His apologies are profuse.'

'Once again?'

'Indeed! Once again!' Jeremy's blond hair flashed in the office lamplight of the dark November morning. 'I must say these large corporations are an absolute bind to deal with. An absolute bind.' He cleared his throat and, looking at the window, avoided my eye for the moment. Such evasion told me that he was not telling me the whole story. I cocked an eye at Geoffrey Price who, pinstriped and white-shirted, was sitting next to me, facing Jeremy. Geoffrey winked back.

'So tell us the rest, Jeremy.' Geoffrey crossed his legs patiently. 'We can guess that no Japanese of any standing would go back on his commitments without a face-saver. How much of their business are we going to handle?'

Jeremy's expression became reluctant. 'He doesn't say.'

'Oh, come on, Jeremy. Spit it out. We've landed some business, haven't we? Tell us the good news.'

'My dear Tim! I really cannot approve, after all that has happened, of your obvious sense of triumph!'

'Jeremy, the Taganoshaganaki Corporation is highly

prestigious. You said so yourself. Don't tell me you won't be strutting about at the next main board meeting, waving your new client at everyone.'

'I do not strut! I have never strutted! Really! You involve yourself in the most—the most seedy of criminal activities, you move about in what can at best only be described as the murkiest fringes of society—no, no, allow me to finish what I'm saying, if you please—you go blaming the innocent Art Fund for these grave misdemeanours—wait! wait!— you—you duff up, yes, that is the only suitable expression— you duff up serious Japanese business executives in the most hooliganic fashion—Tim, will you allow me to finish?—you become even more seriously and deeply *known to the police*, and now you sit smiling blandly across my desk presenting this horrifying series of events as a success. It won't wash, you know. It really will not wash.'

'How much business?' It is always best to ignore Jeremy when he's in one of these moods. One tries to press on with business reality.

He scowled. 'A—um—a proportion, yes, a proportion of some of their overseas investment, particularly the UK investment but also, encouragingly, some of their European business too.'

Geoffrey Price leant forward. 'What proportion?'

'Up to, well, up to ten per cent.'

'Ten per cent!' Geoffrey's pinstripes shot to the vertical. 'Ten per cent! But that's fantastic! That's a hell of a lot of money! Our competitors will be sick with envy. Oh, Tim, well done!'

'*Tim? Tim?*' Jeremy's voice was shrill. 'What do you mean—Tim? What about me? Eh? I did manage to step in and avert an absolute disaster, you know. I did play quite a part!'

'Oh yes, yes, Jeremy, of course, we both know that without you the whole thing would never have come off. Absolutely. Of course.' Geoffrey's tone was soothing, a little too soothing. Jeremy knows those tones. His scowl deepened.

He eyed us both suspiciously from under bristling blond eyebrows. 'I'm glad that you appreciate that.'

'We do, Jeremy. We do.' I smiled broadly.

'Tim! You are an absolute bastard! Really you are! The only consolation to me in all this is that we won't have to buy that bloody Rossetti. I can't stand that sort of thing. I really can't abide it. *Proserpine!* As bad as *Orpheus in the Underworld.* The Art Fund can look elsewhere. We won't have to handle a Rossetti after all, not even as a trade. Thank heavens.'

'Oh no. I'm going to buy a Millais instead.'

'You're going to *what?*'

'Buy a Millais. One should always follow one's own first instincts. It's strange how they so often prove to be the right ones. There's an excellent Millais coming up in the rooms next month. Charles Massenaux alerted me to it. It's one of those lovely Scottish trout-fishing scenes he did, with a man in white clothes casting his fly in a fast-rushing rocky stream in summer. Beautiful. Millais was a great sporting man and his portrait of Ruskin set the scene for that sort of painting. I shall have a real go at that. About two or three hundred thousand.'

Geoffrey Price nodded vigorously. 'That sounds great, Tim. I thoroughly approve. Sporting art is a great investment. And Millais—well, you know my feelings about Millais. The best. One of the very best. Super. I'm so glad that you've decided to go for the soap, rather than the sheep or the goats. Much safer, from an investment point of view. And Jeremy said, didn't he, we must use our cash.' He gave me a meaningful grin, as wide as the Cheshire Cat's.

Jeremy blinked. Suspicion, then reluctant acceptance spread across his face. He spoke grudgingly. 'Well, I suppose if you must, you must. At least Millais is a proper painter. If we have to have a Pre-Raphaelite, if it's absolutely un-avoidable, we should get the least Pre-Raphaelite of the three leaders, I suppose. I do more or less agree with that, so long as it's not one of those frightful, sentimental things. He's as good as Sargent or Orpen, I'm sure.'

'Yes, Jeremy. To be really honest with you I would like more than anything to buy a Holman Hunt as well, but his early paintings are so rare that I don't suppose we'll ever get the opportunity, so you can relax. If one does ever come up, though, look out. I'll be after it.'

He frowned disapprovingly as though the mere thought of a painting by Holman Hunt gave him pain. Then he waved the letter at me. 'I shouldn't tell you this, but do you know what that man Okanura says?'

'No. What?'

He waved the letter again. 'He says that he believes his board will eventually come back round to making an art investment at some point. In those circumstances he would like us to handle the investment for him. He says—and I quote—he says, "I would prefer, if we do make an art investment, which I am sure we will, to have Mr Tim Simpson on our side rather than the opposition."'

I smiled. 'That's very nice of him.'

Jeremy bridled. It's difficult for Jeremy to accept that, despite his most vehement strictures, my thoroughly-condemned activities sometimes work to the Bank's advantage. He gave me a ferocious stare. 'I'm not sure that it is nice of him. Or that it was intended to be so. I really wouldn't be too quick, my dear Tim, to take it as a compliment, if I were you.'

I grinned at Geoffrey. He winked back. Together we faced Jeremy.

'Tubby Postlethwaite would have,' I said.

THE END